A Great Love

A Great Love

ALEXANDRA KOLLONTAI

Translated and introduced by
Cathy Porter

W · W · NORTON & COMPANY
New York   London

Published simultaneously in Canada by George J. McLeod Limited, Toronto.
Printed in the United States of America.

Library of Congress Cataloging in Publication Data
Kollontaï, A. (Aleksandra), 1872–1952.
   A great love.
   Published simultaneously in Canada by George
J. McLeod.
   I. Title.
PG3476.K58A6 1982   891.73'42   81–18696
ISBN 0–393–01595 –5   AACR2
ISBN 0–393–30028–5 (pbk.)

W. W. Norton & Company, Inc. 500 Fifth Avenue, New York, N. Y. 10110
W. W. Norton & Company Ltd. 37 Great Russell Street, London WC1B 3NU

1 2 3 4 5 6 7 8 9 0

Contents

Introduction

In 1923 Alexandra Kollontai's prestige in the Soviet Union was at its lowest. Age-old male prejudice within the Bolshevik Party enabled its new leaders to defame her inspiring views on the new sexual morality by attaching them in people's minds to her crimes as a 'deviationist' – her belief that workers should control the new economy for which they had made the revolution, her support in 1921 of the Workers' Opposition, and her stand against the New Economic Policy (N E P). Her able leadership of the Party Women's Department was labelled incompetent and she was relieved of her post as its director. Her writings on sexuality and revolution were attacked as scandalous, as was her personal life. Her marriage shortly after the revolution to Pavel Dybenko, a sailor of peasant origin much younger than she, had exposed a nasty vein of class snobbery and sexual puritanism within the Party, and she had compounded her crime by interceding for him when he was thrown into a Bolshevik jail for insubordination.

We may now feel that the weakest point in Kollontai's thinking was her failure explicitly to connect her ideas on women's control over their lives and bodies and workers' control over the economy; but this implicit connection was not lost on those who came to power after Lenin's last illness. In 1922 she was assigned work outside Russia by Stalin, then acting secretary of the Party; by 1923 her liberating vision of happier and freer relationships between men and women was denounced as 'bourgeois' and 'decadent', and yet more slanderous epithets were invoked in years to come. And so Kollontai became one more culprit singled out by Stalin to justify a society in moral and economic crisis.

But, ironically, it seems that in this most crushing and hopeless period of her life male prejudice may have helped her. For she was not forced publicly to recant her views (already adequately slandered by propaganda), and was not subjected to any punishment more dreadful than being ignored in a safe but lonely diplomatic post in Scandinavia. She left Russia at the end of 1922. At the age of fifty-two, with her political life in Russia over and her great love for Dybenko collapsing, she started a new life in Oslo. It was then that she turned to fiction to express some of the hopes and conflicts of women in revolution.

In her more political writings after the N E P of 1921 she had shown how dwindling crêches and rising female unemployment were gradually driving women back into the economic dependence and isolation of marriage or the miseries of prostitution. In her fiction she revealed her insights into women's lives before and after the revolution, and a confidence, born of experience, that women would support one another as they explored new ways to bring up their children, organise their work, live with and love men as their equals. In *Love of Worker Bees* and *A Great Love* (both written in Oslo in 1922 and published the following year), she showed women resisting the insidious psychological and economic pressures which were so deeply rooted in the N E P. Her characters grow in the painful process of challenging their old oppressive dependence on men; they leave us at the point of abandoning lovers, and relationships they feel unable to transform, in order first to transform themselves, fight for their dignity, and find the confidence to make new independent lives for themselves.

Elsewhere, in her non-fiction writing, she had already examined how society creates some of the tensions women experience as lovers, mothers and workers, in their sexual needs and their social relationships. To suggest that women are doomed for all time to this psychic dislocation between passion and politics would, she felt, be to reinforce all sorts of depressingly conventional ideas they have of their incompleteness, their inability to 'connect'. History has created these tensions within all of us, suggests Kollontai, but in ways that are experienced particularly painfully by women. So it is they who must work out new ways of living which will best suit their needs; only then will the 'great love' she envisaged become a reality.

The women characters in these stories (subtitled 'Studies in the Psychology of Women') are intellectuals, more educated and articulate than those in *Love of Worker Bees*, and also more isolated from each other, more apt to internalise. Politics and the Party are in the background, men are mere emotional shadows. Women's personal experiences are the stories' starting-point, and they have the narrative voice.

The title story, the longest and most important, is set shortly after Russia's 1905 revolution, 'far away and long ago in the dim and distant past, long before the world had experienced the bloody horrors of the First World War or the mighty upheavals of the Bolshevik revolution'. By 1907 hundreds of workers and revolutionaries had been imprisoned and exiled, and by 1908 Kollontai too was wanted by the police. She fled to Germany and there began to assess some of the complex questions raised by the failure of that first heroic revolution and the possibilities of a second successful one. There, at a distance from the struggle, she began to see how the politics of the underground had split people's consciousness and created a false dualism between the 'selfish' life of introspection and the 'virtuous' life of the collective. She knew the two were interdependent, for social change must proceed from a change in people's psyche, and revolutionaries' talk of the wonderful socialist collective of the future would be worth nothing if it was composed of lifeless individuals with neither passion nor complexity.

1905 had offered a glimpse of this new collective living, but it was one in which people felt more real to each other in fighting than in loving and caring for one another. Savage tsarist repression had produced a particularly hard-line style of underground politics, a rigid analysis of the class struggle and an intimidating stress on the intellectual brilliance needed for factional debates. All this operated particularly harshly against women in the revolutionary movement, especially a woman like Kollontai who had a young child to care for on her own. It was in the eight years she lived as an exile in the West, where the collective was less developed than in Russia and the individual more highly valued, that Kollontai began to insist more boldly that the Russian revolutionary movement must broaden its aspirations to include the more personal desires of the men and women *making* that revolution.

The old form of the family, which had so enslaved women and submerged their sexuality, was also in revolution; people were already evolving radically new attitudes to sexual morality; there was nothing utopian in calling for a revolution of the human psyche. She saw that personal life does not conveniently 'recede' at moments of great social upheaval, as so many still claim it does. On the contrary, as her own life would indicate, people experience happiness and tragedy in particularly intense and entangled ways at the great historical turning-points of which revolutions are made.

In the years between 1908 and 1917, as she travelled around speaking at factory and trade-union meetings in Germany, where she was based, and in England, Belgium,

France, Scandinavia, Switzerland and America, she wrote her first articles on sexuality and revolution. As she read the works of Havelock Ellis and of various pioneering Swiss and German psychologists (including possibly Freud), she was gradually drawn to a more 'individualist interpretation of human behaviour than was acceptable to the predominantly male revolutionary movement in Russia. The stories she wrote some eleven years later explore some of her more complex insights into relationships in revolution than do the articles she wrote in those years.

The title story is partly a projection of her own experiences then. At some point in 1909 she became involved with a Russian economist named Maslov, also an exile, who was wandering around Europe with his wife and numerous children. The illicit nature of the affair and Maslov's attachment to a marriage that made him and his wife so unhappy exasperated her, and in 1910 she escaped to Paris for a while to be alone and write. There was a particular passion about the articles she wrote there, in which she denounced the ourtworn old marriage and looked forward to the time when men and women could love without imprisoning, fearing and oppressing one another.

Kollontai and Maslov successfully guarded their privacy. But what becomes clear in *A Great Love* was that she had discovered important aspects of her own situation in the lives of three Russian revolutionaries also based in Paris at that time – Lenin, his wife Nadezhda Krupskaya and Inessa Armand, a French-born Bolshevik woman staying with them there. It is possible that Kollontai read more into their relationship than was warranted, since she met them only briefly in Paris, but it is equally likely that Armand revealed details of it to her when the two became friendly after the Bolshevik revolution. There is at any rate overwhelming evidence that *A Great Love* is a *roman à clef*.

When the work was first published in Russia, though, few

would have wanted to recognise Lenin in the dull and devious Senya, a ruthless, selfish, pedantic bore, constantly preoccupied with his latest article and plagued with minor illnesses, money worries and marriage problems. Only when the story was republished in 1927 – and later, shortly after Krupskaya's death in 1939 and the publication of Lenin's more intimate letters to Armand – did it become clear that Kollontai most probably had been close to the truth of the affair. She certainly gives Senya some of Lenin's bounce, humour and authority, even his cap and his beard (although Senya, unlike the childless Lenin, was a devoted father, as apparently was Maslov). In general, though, he is a deeply unattractive character. It would also be hard to recognise Krupskaya, a gentle and intelligent woman, in Senya's tedious ailing wife Anyuta (here again Kollontai probably had Maslov's wife partly in mind), although Krupskaya did, like Anyuta, have a bad heart and weak nerves which Lenin was always anxious not to excite. Natasha, on the other hand, like Kollontai and Armand, was a 'new woman', who had broken with conventional marriage and now had a past to answer for.

It was during the 1905 revolution that both Kollontai and Armand became most painfully conscious of the double standard in sexual morality – and of all the various other ways men subordinated women's needs in the revolutionary movement. Kollontai was living in St Petersburg at that time, while Armand was in Moscow. They were isolated geographically from one another, and, as two of the extremely small number of full-time women revolutionaries – and single mothers at that – they were also isolated from the movement in ways they could not have articulated at the time. Kollontai and Armand met only fleetingly in Paris in 1911, got to know each other well only after the Bolshevik revolution, and even then civil war, illness and work in different towns separated them. But there were striking affinities between them; enough for Kollontai to feel justified, after Armand's death, in speculating about her early experiences. For like Kollontai, Armand was a child of the old liberal tsarist culture, a vital and generous woman who had explored her own sexual freedom and wanted to integrate a radically new sexual politics into the class politics of the Russian underground.

Evidence for a sexual relationship between Armand and Lenin is circumstantial, and it is always possible they were not actually lovers. Bolsheviks close to them at the time have of course treated the matter with enormous caution, whilst the Russian and French police routinely referred to Armand as 'Lenin's mistress'. (But then Kollontai was also so described when arrested in Russia shortly before the Bolshevik revolution). The publication of *A Great Love* certainly roused great interest amongst many western scholars anxious to discredit Lenin with a less than perfectly monogamous life. Armand's biographer Jean Fréville, on the other hand, merely answers the question rhetorically: 'how could Lenin not be seduced by this exceptional being, who combined intelligence with such beauty, energy with femininity, practical sense with revolutionary ardour?' *A Great Love*, however, although probably based more on imaginative speculation than on close intimacy with the situation, does suggest very convincingly that they were indeed lovers at some point.

Born in 1874 of a French father and an English mother, Inessa Armand was two years younger than Kollontai; her upbringing was more unconventional. Her parents were actors who had settled in Russia, and were touring the theatres of France at the time their second child was born. Her father died shortly afterwards, and her mother, penniless and desperate, took her back to Russia to live with her maternal grandmother, who was working as a governess for a wealthier branch of the Armand family in Moscow.

Inessa was much loved and well educated by her liberal benefactors, under whose kindly influence she became deeply religious and (like Nadezhda Krupskaya and many other women radicals of the 1880s and 90s) a devout Tolstoyan. By the age of eighteen she had qualified as a governess. She never put her precious teaching certificate to use however, for before the year was out she had married the eldest Armand son, Alexander, a wealthy businessman of great generosity and liberal inclinations. Over the next seven years she bore four children, two girls and two boys.

Armand first became politically active in 1900, when she joined a women's charity organisation in Moscow, the Society for Improving the Lot of Women, and worked with the branch formed to rehabilitate prostitutes. A letter she wrote to Tolstoy on this painful question received the shocking response 'Thus it was before Moses; thus it shall always be.' After this infuriating piece of wisdom, Armand could no longer be content with her old vague Tolstoyan liberalism, and began to explore more practical and radical solutions to the whole woman question. She grew increasingly restless in her life with Alexander and by the time her fifth child, a son, was born in Switzerland, she had lost her religious faith and her marriage was in crisis. She had also fallen deeply in love with Alexander's younger more radical brother Vladimir (who may possibly have been the father of her youngest child.) Shortly after returning to Moscow she left Alexander – they remained close friends – and she and her five children moved in with Vladimir. Alexander supported them all financially throughout his life.

In December 1905 Armand played an active part in the Moscow uprising, after which her flat and her movements came under constant police surveillance. When she was finally arrested in 1907 it was as a Socialist Revolutionary (a non-marxist who had inherited the terrorist traditions of the 1880s and regarded the peasants, not the factory-workers, as the agents of revolution in Russia.) But this charge on her dossier was unlikely to have been a very accurate description of her politics, and most probably she had no party affiliations at this time. Leaving her children with Alexander she set off for exile in Archangel, accompanied by the heroic Vladimir. But he was soon so sick with tuberculosis that he was forced to leave for Switzerland. She remained in Archangel without him for a year, before finally managing to escape via Finland to join him. Shortly after her arrival he died. Distraught with grief, she moved quickly to Brussels where she tried to apply herself to the study of pedagogics, but her depression was too devastating and nothing could hold her attention. She may have met Lenin briefly at some point in this most hopeless period of her life. But it was only in October 1910, when she moved to Paris, the home of so many wandering Russian exiles, that she became close friends with him and Krupskaya. She rented a small cheap flat near theirs, arranged for her three eldest children to join her there, and was soon a full-time political activist, one of the leading and most passionate of the Paris Leninists and an ardent champion of women's emancipation.

It was in June 1911 that Kollontai first met her, Lenin and Krupskaya, and the memories of that summer were still vivid for her twelve years later when she wrote *A Great Love*. While Kollontai was staying alone in Paris to write, Armand was teaching at Lenin's summer school in the little village of Lonjumeau, near Paris (she was the only woman to be so honoured), and staying in the school building there with her children. Kollontai saw her and other Bolsheviks at various meetings for which they cycled into Paris every day. Although Kollontai herself was a Menshevik at that time and had deep reservations about the Bolshevik leadership, she was not excessively worried by the factional differences between them, and could not but be impressed by the Bolsheviks' cheerful confidence and evident popularity in Paris.

Kollontai too was an extremely popular figure amongst the rather anarchic Russian community in Paris. It was surely her own experiences as a revolutionary that prompted her to speculate about some of the ways Inessa Armand might have experienced her subordination to Lenin's authority. In *A Great Love,* Natasha grows to know herself in recognising that her support for Senya, and her loyal performance of the secretarial tasks he assigns her, are burying other talents, smothering her enthusiasm and passion, and slowly killing her 'great love' for him. He takes her devotion to him for granted and returns it with resentment and suspicion; he imposes unendurable psychological burdens on her: 'She could never allow herself to be weak with him, she knew that, for she had not only her own problems to cope with but his as well. She had to bear the entire psychological burden for both of them, in fact. She was his support, his consolation, his ray of hope, his joy – yes, she must always bring him joy, for with Anyuta it was nothing but grief, tears and endless anxieties. With her it must be a perpetual holiday, fun and laughter all the time.'

Again and again he belittles the importance of her political work and is jealous of her and her relationships with others in the Party. When for the hundredth time she bites back her words to him – for he will not listen – she realises with gradually diminishing pain what a very small place she occupies in his view of the world: 'He was somehow deaf and blind to her, he saw her only in profile, never head-on as a whole person, as she really was ... She was a silhouette whose contours he himself had drawn, for that was all he was interested in knowing or seeing of her.' Painfully she makes herself recognise how insensitive he is to her sexual needs and her need to work, her political aspirations and the state

16

of her finances. She feels imprisoned by the secrecy of their relationship and the boredom and isolation it brings her, exhausted by the suppressed anger and half-truths that lie beneath the surface of their time together, so that she felt sometimes 'a strain so exhausting that she would often breathe a secret sigh of relief when he'd gone, and she could return, unhindered, to her own thoughts and moods'. The story concludes as Natasha steps on to the train that will take her away from Senya for ever, bravely preparing to face solitude and danger in her new life in the underground. By then, 'the great love which had made her heart beat all those years which she thought would never fade, had gone forever ... Nothing, no tenderness, no prayers, not even understanding, could reawaken it'.

In describing the tensions in Senya and Natasha's relationship Kollontai was writing out of experiences shared by every woman revolutionary at the time, particularly those, like Armand, in the Bolshevik faction. For by 1910 the Bolsheviks were at a turning-point and were at last gaining real strength. It was at this most militant and hopeful period of their history that attitudes to women's organisation and sexual politics emerged which would set the tone for the passionate discussion of these issues after the Bolshevik revolution. In these discussions, Kollontai and Armand were the leading radical voices, while the more conservative Krupskaya, whose reverence for marriage revealed a rather more puritanical attitude to sex, talked more of women's literacy programmes and housework-sharing than of sexuality and communal childcare. Yet despite Armand's almost intimidatingly liberated way of life and her closeness to Lenin, there was much that drew her and Krupskaya together in a friendship that lasted from 1910 to Armand's death ten years later.

After the Longjumeau school ended in the late summer of 1911, Armand moved back to her Paris flat with her three children, and was shortly afterwards appointed by Lenin to a leading Party post, as secretary of the Committee of Emigré Organisations. 'We saw Inessa every day,' Krupskaya later recalled in her memoirs, 'and she became very close to us. She loved my old mother very much.' Although the friendship between the two women is not an aspect of the relationship Kollontai deals with in *A Great Love*, she does indicate some shared experiences: the way both these women, like so many others in the revolutionary movement then and in years to come, learnt to stifle their own initiative in the supposedly larger interests of 'class unity' and a united party. At several points in the story she suggests how women's interests are subordinated and ignored by a party which finds them so threateningly divisive. As, for example, when Natasha, who has left work in her home town to stay with Senya, is urgently summoned back. 'Yes,' retorts Senya, 'and who is that writing? Maria Mikhailovna? I might have known! She's nothing but an hysterical woman who's always moaning about something . . . Who gives a toss what *she* thinks!'

In fact, about half the forty or so Bolsheviks living in Paris in 1910 were women. Krupskaya was editorial secretary of the Bolsheviks' newspaper; Armand was in charge of all the correspondence between the numerous emigré Bolshevik communities scattered around Europe; and many other women there were doing equally complicated and responsible jobs for the Party. It seemed perfectly natural to Armand and Krupskaya, therefore, to combine this work with some political women's meetings for the French and Russian milliners, dressmakers and servants in the city. A few meetings did take place, with Lenin's support, but their organisers were soon encountering such ferocious opposition from most of the men in the Bolshevik community that the scheme was eventually dropped.

This incident is from Krupskaya's memoirs of 1910. There

18

were other conflicts she must have experienced with Armand, her friend and her rival for Lenin's love, about which she was understandably more reticent, and Soviet historians have been equally reticent about such intimate matters. There is virtually only one episode which has been omitted from the scrupulous Soviet documentation of Lenin's life, and that is in the spring of 1912. In May that year, Armand travelled south from Paris to Bordeaux. Subsequent events make it reasonable to suppose that Lenin joined her in the little town of Arcachon a few days later, and stayed with her there for a week or so. Kollontai was possibly claiming to know more than she did when she confided later to her French secretary that Krupskaya had offered to leave Lenin at this point, and that he had begged her to stay. But in *A Great Love*, the imaginative amplification she gives to this clandestine holiday sounds quite plausible, and the south of France provides the 'burning tropical landscape' in which Senya and Natasha enjoy the first summer of their love together.

For Lenin and Armand, however, these days evidently spelt the end of the first phase of their love affair. Immediately afterwards Lenin, Krupskaya and her mother moved to Poland, and Armand returned recklessly to Russia as an underground agent. It is on a rather similar note that *A Great Love* ends, just as Natasha is facing all the excitements and dangers of her new independent life. Armand's move seems to have been prompted more by desperation than good sense, and few doubted that the combined intelligence of the Russian and French police would land her in prison the moment she set foot in Russia. Gathering up her children in Paris, she travelled to Cracow, where she stopped for a few days with Lenin and Krupskaya before embarking on the journey back to Russia. As her friends had predicted, she was arrested almost immediately and thrown into jail, where she developed the first symptoms of tuberculosis.

It was a year before her loving husband succeeded in bailing her out. She fled the country immediately, and by September 1913 she had joined Lenin and Krupskaya in Poland. Armand's courage in returning to Russia and her experiences there evidently endeared her to Krupskaya, and Armand herself apparently made efforts to strengthen a friendship which had been so clouded with rivalry. 'Inessa told me a great deal about her life and her children, and there was a delightful warmth in her stories,' Krupskaya recalled. 'Illich and I went for long walks with her.' Once again, Armand rented a room in a house near theirs. The shared political work and long walks in the country continued, and Armand, herself an excellent pianist, even persuaded the unmusical Lenins to accompany her to a cycle of Beethoven concerts. While Lenin and his close friend Lev Kamenev (in whose house she was staying) focused their attention on the mounting wave of angry strikes and demonstrations in Russia, she had her own exciting first-hand observations of life there to share with Krupskaya and Kamenev's wife Lilina. By now it was clear that women strikers, particularly in the textile unions, were a force the Bolsheviks could no longer afford to ignore.

Earlier in 1913, when women workers in the cities started planning demonstrations for a new socialist holiday, International Women's Day, it was Krupskaya who had suggested that the Bolsheviks' paper *Pravda* publish a special women's issue. Leading European and Russian socialists, including Kollontai, wrote articles on the political significance of Women's Day demonstrations in tsarist Russia, and March 8 that year was celebrated there with huge women's meetings and parades in which countless women were arrested. Inspired by the letters which then poured into *Pravda* from women all over Russia, Krupskaya and

Armand began putting together some ideas for a new Bolshevik women's paper.

For a while Armand settled happily into her new life in Cracow, and even contemplated sending for her children to join her there. But this small emigré world soon became oppressive and in December 1913 she moved back to Paris, where she stayed until war broke out the following year. She resumed her secretarial work for the Paris-based Bolshevik Emigré Organisation, and in January 1914 she joined Kollontai as a Russian delegate to the Socialist International Women's Bureau. She and another Bolshevik woman in Paris wrote regularly to Krupskaya and Lilina in Cracow, and it was from these women's correspondence with four other women in St Petersburg that plans for a Bolshevik women's paper eventually took shape.

The letters Armand wrote to Krupskaya are friendly and businesslike, alternating between the formal and the intimate 'you' form. None of her letters to Lenin at this time have been published, but of those he wrote to her after her departure from Cracow, twenty were published after Krupskaya's death. Informal and friendly, he addressed her throughout in the intimate 'you' form, which he used only for relatives and a few close friends. They probably met only once during this time, in January 1914, when Lenin visited Paris alone for a week and was invited by Armand to give a talk to Paris socialists on the subject of Bloody Sunday and the 1905 revolution.

Incredibly, despite much resistance from the Bolshevik leadership, and the distance and communication difficulties between the three groups of women in Paris, Cracow and St Petersburg, they did manage to establish an editorial board of sorts and, on March 8 1914, to produce the first issue of their new paper, *Woman Worker*. But the outbreak of war five months later put paid to this, as to so many other projects. As Russian exiles fled to the neutral countries and formed new political alliances, the Bolsheviks, virtually the only socialist group in Europe consistently to oppose the slaughter, gained hundreds of new members – including Alexandra Kollontai. Immediately after war was declared, Lenin and Krupskaya moved from Poland to the small Swiss town of Berne, where they were soon joined by Armand. She rented a flat near theirs, and her company was a comfort to Krupskaya in these terrible times. Later Krupskaya would recall the long peaceful evenings when Armand played the piano and she and Lenin busied themselves with their correspondence, and the long walks they all took together to pick mushrooms or 'sit on some sunny wooded hillside, Ilich making notes for an article, me studying my Italian, and Inessa sewing a skirt in the autumn sunshine'.

Yet according to one western scholar at least, 'it was widely taken for granted by socialists who knew Lenin that Armand was his mistress in 1915'. It is possible. It is also possible that when in January 1916 Armand returned to Paris with a forged passport to establish contact with French anti-war leftists, she had left Lenin for good. For when she went back to Switzerland again she lived first in one town, then in another, and saw Lenin only once, at a conference.

There is a sad final comment on their relationship, in two letters Lenin wrote to her in 1915. Armand had for some time been developing ideas for a pamphlet she wanted to write for young people in Russian – and particularly for her own teenage daughters – on sexual morality. First, though, she decided to ask Lenin for some advice, rather as she had turned to Tolstoy fifteen years earlier. How, Lenin demanded in his replies (her original letters to him have not been published) could she possibly claim that 'even a transient passion is "purer" and "more poetic" than the "loveless kisses" between philistine (oh so philistine!) spouses?' Such talk of women's emancipation and sexual freedom went with particularly pernicious notions of bour-

geois morality (he made this point several times); demand
freedom from social and religious prejudice by all means, but
freedom from 'seriousness in love' was no freedom at all. No,
women's sexual liberation would be a perfectly natural
consequence of the socialist society and its revolutionary
new marriage laws, which would introduce a 'proletarian
civil marriage, based on love. (And add, *but only if you
absolutely must*, that "fleeting liaisons can be pure, and they
can be base").'

Armand never wrote her pamphlet Whether or not
Kollontai ever saw it in draft form, she must have recognised
Armand as an ally, whose radical views on sexual matters
were quite unacceptable to Bolshevik orthodoxy. They met
for the second time in Petrograd, in dramatic circumstances,
shortly after Kollontai had returned to Russia from exile and
two months after the first, February, revolution of 1917. In
April Armand, Lenin and Krupskaya travelled with a large
party of Bolsheviks across Europe in the famous sealed train
which bore them in triumph to the Finland Station;
Kollontai was amongst the rapturous supporters who met
them there. Armand immediately moved back to her old
base in Moscow where she was soon a leading Bolshevik
activist. Kollontai, whose status in the Party was also
extremely high at that time, was still alone in urging the
Bolsheviks to set up a special bureau, run by women, to deal
specifically with women's issues. Her proposal was greeted
very defensively, and it was only with great reluctance that
Lenin agreed that she present the idea 'strictly on her own
initiative' to a forthcoming Party conference. To her
mortification, her scheme was rejected outright by every
leading Bolshevik woman there. Even Armand felt, apparently with some reservations, that since the Party now
seemed strong enough to make a revolution that would
automatically wipe out all forms of oppression, organising
women's groups would be impractical, politically incorrect,

and bound to introduce 'sexual divisions' into the grand ideal of the united Party.

Since most leading women activists naturally found their constituency amongst women factory-workers and soldiers' wives, however, this extreme 'anti-feminism' must have lain uneasily with their commitment to the various issues concerning the working women they met. It was only after the Bolshevik revolution of October 1917 that Armand began to argue, more circumspectly than Kollontai, for a Party women's bureau based on the German model.

She had met Lenin and Krupskaya only very fleetingly since their return to Russia, and by then passion had apparently settled into deep friendship on all sides. In the summer of 1918 Lenin was shot, and thought for a while to be dying. The first and virtually the only person he called for in his convalescence was Armand, who arrived with her teenage daughter Varvara to see him. While Krupskaya and Varvara exchanged old photographs she and Lenin talked, and after his recovery and return to work he was endlessly attentive to her needs and those of her children in those terrible days.

Through civil war, social chaos and famine, as marriages collapsed and passions withered under the strains of shared hardship, both Armand and Kollontai strove for radical clarity on the position of women in Russia. Forced separations were setting men free to form new liaisons in other towns and leaving women to work, support their children and fight for their rations; state canteens and crêches were hopelessly inadequate. The women's congress Armand and Kollontai helped organise in Moscow in November 1918 was a major breakthrough in encouraging women to raise before the Party some of the desperate material and psychological problems besetting them. The popularity of the congress exceeded all expectations: over a thousand red-kerchiefed women crossed the war-zones to arrive, hungry and exhausted, in Moscow. There they listened as Armand, in a furious diatribe against pots and pans and women's isolated drudgery at home, demanded that the government set up more canteens and nurseries. She sat down to worried cries of 'But we won't give up our children!', and Kollontai then gave her famous speech on communism and the family. Assuring women that the Bolsheviks had no intention of separating them from their children, she urged that as the old family collapsed to be replaced by something better, women should push the new government into ensuring that the process was not made too painful for them, and outlined the better times they could look forward to after the civil war ended.

It was at last decided that every Party organisation should have its own women's commission, to be supervised by Kollontai, Armand and one other woman. Armand and Kollontai worked together for a couple of months, but in December 1918 Kollontai was confined to bed with a heart complaint until the following March, and shortly after that she was sent off on an exhausting six-month propaganda tour of the Southern Front. Meanwhile Armand set up meetings throughout Russia at which women elected Party, union and government delegates who learnt how the government worked and how to make it work for them. These meetings were so well attended that soon virtually every province in European Russia had its own women's commission, and in September 1919 the commission was upgraded to a Party Women's Department, centrally directed by Armand.

It came as a surprise to many that the more radical Kollontai, who returned to Moscow that month, was passed over in the leadership. But her post as women's organiser in the countryside was a crucial one, and at meetings all over Russia women gradually began to discuss the long ignored questions of abortion and alimony, venereal disease and prostitution. But the Women's Department was also gaining enemies. When Kollontai and Armand started organising an international conference of communist women for the following summer, they encountered such opposition that they felt impelled to petition the Party Central Committee on 'the pressing problem of the Women's Department's relationship with the trade unions, in view of the heated discussions on this matter which are badly disrupting our work'.

Both women were unsupported, overworked and ill. By October Kollontai had contracted typhus and became delirious for a while. For the next eight months Armand heroically struggled on alone, often working a sixteen-hour day at the Women's Department. Only occasionally did she complain about her cramped and noisy office ('our comrades, especially those in the Women's Department, do so love to chat'), and run off to the unheated public library to work alone. It was an impoverished and lonely life. Her four oldest children were all working as Party militants in other towns and only her youngest son was in Moscow, staying with relatives. She lived alone in one small cold room, and saw little of her old friends. But when she eventually contracted pneumonia in February 1920, it was Lenin who personally ensured that her food and firewood rations were increased. He also had a telephone installed in her room (a rare luxury for a private citizen in those days), and insisted that her young son 'phone him every day with news of her health.

Painfully thin and ravaged by illness, she returned to work in the late spring of 1920. Since both Kollontai and the German women's organiser Clara Zetkin were also ill at this time, she drafted single-handed all the resolutions for the forthcoming international women's conference, and by the time it was over in June she was too ill to do anything more. One of her older sons, a Red Army pilot, was also ill, and at Lenin's insistence, they both set off in September for the Caucasus to recuperate. They arrived in Kislovodsk, Armand more dead than alive, her son already well on the mend, to find a White guerilla force encircling the town. Leading Party workers there had received instructions from Lenin to look after them, and the Red Army commander who met them off the train had orders to remove them, bodily if necessary, from the danger. The spa was closed down, the ailing patients were loaded into slow trains, and after several days' travelling and a two-day delay in a filthy small station filled with sick evacuees, they finally arrived at their destination, a small northern town further up the mountains. For several days Armand wandered restlessly about the mountains, driven by a desire for privacy. Then she collapsed, succumbed to the cholera epidemic which was sweeping the country, and died a few days later in the hospital there.

In October Kollontai rose from her sick bed to join the Central Committee and Armand's many friends to meet the coffin at Moscow's Kazan Station. Her body lay in state for twenty-four hours before being escorted to the Kremlin walls by a procession of mourners, softly singing the Funeral March. As the ashes were being interred, Lenin appeared. His face, Kollontai later recalled, was virtually covered by a thick scarf which concealed his tears. 'He was unrecognisable,' she told her secretary. 'He walked with closed eyes and we thought at any moment he would collapse. He never survived Inessa's death, and it was this that precipitated the illnesses which eventually undermined him too.'

When *A Great Love* was first published in 1923, a year before Lenin's death, Kollontai must have felt it had a relevance beyond that involving him, Armand and Krupskaya. Four years later Stalin's campaign against the idealists of the revolution was at its height and the ageing Krupskaya, who had been courageously defending the Party against the horrors being perpetrated in Lenin's name, was singled out as a special target of attack. In 1927, while the rest of Kollontai's writings were all but buried under a mass of crude defamatory attacks and she herself was out of the country, the title story was seized on as a handy weapon against Krupskaya, and republished.

This sad sequel, one more blow to revolutionary hopes, raises questions as to how Kollontai saw her own part in this vile campaign. Yet the core of optimism in her life and writings still survives for us. She knew that visions of the possibilities within us and of the better life to come are fragile, but that these insights may be the most real things we know – and that the chasm between our lives as they are and our desires for the future *can* be crossed. Like feminists now, she believed that the crippling separation women experience between work and love, economics and biology, must be described before it can be resolved, and that fiction may be one of the best ways to present the reality of this experience. She wrote in her essay *The New Woman* 'The less harsh reality is romanticised and the more fully and truthfully contemporary woman's psychology is presented, with all her struggles, migraines and aspirations, all her problems, contradictions and complexity, the richer the material for the spiritual image of the new woman we shall have to study'.

Kollontai saw that in defining themselves and helping to make a better society, women must for a time make work, not love, the centre of their lives. But by 1922, as she ended her love affair with Dybenko, came to terms with her political isolation in Scandinavia and started writing *A Great Love*, she had already learnt from painful experience that this sad choice, which weighs so heavily on women, is generally prompted by despair, and that the price women must pay for being strong is often solitude, uncertainty and ridicule. Surely, too, she saw beyond this choice to more tragic and universal conflicts between the personal and the political. She certainly suggested more complexity in people's relationships and more diversity in their options and experiences than was acceptable in the Soviet Union when these stories first came out. I think they will touch on many sensitive nerves now.

Cathy Porter, London 1980

A Great Love

A Great Love

All this happened far away and long ago in the dim and distant past, long before the world had experienced the bloody horrors of the First World War or the mighty upheavals of the Bolshevik revolution. It happened in the years of the savage Tsarist reaction which followed the revolution of 1905, and the story concerns a group of revolutionaries living in exile in France. Since then a new world has dawned in Russia, but we may see elements of the story repeating themselves in our lives, and perhaps by learning something about the characters here we may learn something about ourselves too ...

It was seven long months since she'd last seen him. Seven months ago they'd parted, and both had decided the parting would be the final one.

'It's all over now,' they'd agreed, 'this is the end.' And he'd buried his head on her shoulder, closed his eyes and confessed to her how unbearable it was and how defeated he felt. His face had seemed so touchingly childlike, so thin, and so infinitely precious.

'You see, the moment the doctor diagnosed her illness as a heart condition,' (he was talking about his wife) 'I felt like a criminal, a butcher, and I knew I couldn't go on doing this to her. Her life's been hard enough as it is – I couldn't bear

31

to think I was adding to her troubles. I suppose I feel I must do all I can to see she stays reasonably healthy – can you understand that, Natasha dear ... ? And then I thought about the children – how could I lie to them? Why, Sasha's old enough now to understand everything; and nothing escapes those knowing eyes of his. I do think it's so important for the children to feel their father is there when they need him.'

'But do you really think it'll be that easy to forget the past and all that we've meant to each other?' Natasha had ventured to ask (she was, as always, considering his needs first). 'Will you ever be able to forget how close we've been, the way we understand every look and word between us, everything we've done together ... ? How will you be able simply to go back to your family? Won't you feel dreadfully lonely?'

'Yes, of course I shall, unspeakably lonely; life will be utterly grim and depressing and I shall be wretched,' he clasped her tighter, 'but what else can we do?'

Then restlessly, as if trying to banish these dark premonitions from his mind, he had begun to cover her body with kisses, embracing her with an intensity which both excited and frightened her, and somehow left her feeling afterwards that she no longer understood him. At such a time, feeling such pain at the prospect of losing him, she longed for the comfort of his kisses and naturally she hadn't resisted. Yet his caresses that night had been painful, excessive, and later she'd felt somehow insulted by them, abused.

It was pouring with rain the next morning, the day they had to part. Her train was leaving earlier than his, and she left him lying asleep. As she collected her things and packed her bag she moved around the room mechanically, her mind a blank, all feelings frozen, locked up deep inside her. It was strange to see him still sleeping there, calm and untroubled, in the bed they'd shared.

She finished her packing, put on her hat and adjusted her veil, slung her travelling bag across her shoulder and went over to sit beside him on the edge of the bed. He started up, suddenly wide awake. 'Not leaving already, are you?' Her silent response was to stroke his forehead and hair, as if he were a sick child she was trying to comfort.

'Why d'you have to rush off at this hour of the morning? Look, there's no earthly reason why you should leave now when there's an evening train you can catch – won't you stay with me until then?' But as Natasha knew all too well, he had been spoilt by the love and rivalry of two women, and now he thought he could always get his own way. At any other time this spontaneous way he had of changing plans, this desire to be with her a little longer – if only for one more hour – would have filled her with joy. But on that cold wet morning of their final parting she was amazed that he could be so capricious and so demanding.

'You know quite well why I'm hurrying. If I leave this evening I shall miss the opening session of our Party congress.'

'Oh, come on now! It won't be such a tragedy if you're a little late! They'll manage very nicely without you, you know.' Moving closer to her he'd started to nibble her ear and then, with mounting passion, to kiss her neck. But she hadn't responded. His words had stung her and she thought of all the other occasions when he'd referred so disparagingly to her work for the Party – *their* Party; she wondered if he'd ever understand that it was only out of a sense of total commitment to her political work that she derived the strength to endure their separation for good.

So she had left to catch the train which was to carry her away from him for ever. Gazing through the film of rain on the compartment window at the unfamiliar scenery flashing past her she tried to shake off the painful anxiety which had settled in her heart, throbbing dully, like toothache. The contemptuous way he'd referred to her work, that remark of his that her Party comrades would 'manage very nicely without her' had overshadowed the agony of this last parting. Why, he attached absolutely no importance at all to her work and the huge amount of energy she put into it! As far as he saw it her work was expendable!

It was only as dusk was falling and the compartment emptied that she had begun to cry about him; she cried for those wonderful intelligent eyes of his which she would never see again, and for that childish grin which so often lit up the stern face of a man who was, after all, an *authority*, a figure of power in the revolutionary circles in which they both moved.

When parting, they had both solemnly sworn to break off all communication; there were to be no letters, no attempts to meet. When Natasha had said 'Never, never forget that I shall be somewhere on this earth, and that if you should ever need me ... ' she didn't have to finish; he understood her and was grateful. Nevertheless, when the actual moment came for her to leave she'd been unable to believe it was really happening, just as we can never believe it when someone we love is about to die.

It wasn't as if it had been their first attempt to end things. But invariably, on those previous occasions, before three weeks were up she'd receive a telegram from him, an abject letter, some sort of message in which he'd beg her to take him back, tell her how much he loved her, missed her, longed for her. And then of course his political work suffered without her, for he knew nobody else with whom he could talk so freely and at such length about his ideas; he might want to talk about the thesis of some Party document he was thinking about or sometimes it was a particular political campaign he felt an urgent need to discuss with her. In fact on quite a few occasions after these solemn partings she would receive a letter from him out of the blue which contained not one single reference to her, but merely described whatever agonising intellectual problems he happened to be struggling with at the time. It was just like the continuation of some political argument. It was only at the very end of these letters that he'd make his usual appeal for another meeting; he needed her, he'd say – and of course that was true.

After this last 'final parting' of theirs, however, day followed day, week followed week, and still there was no word, no telegram from him ...

Natasha had gone straight back to work after leaving him. At first she'd been able to think of little but her own aching loneliness, and had struggled with feelings of utter uselessness and indifference to the work that had been so important to her. But she became absorbed in it again soon enough. She re-established contact with her Party comrades, all of them committed to the same values, and before long she was so happy to be working with her friends that sometimes she'd suddenly realise that she hadn't so much as thought about him all day. She forgot to miss him – and she really didn't know whether to feel pleased or disturbed.

It was only after some particularly nerve-racking day at work, returning late at night to her small solitary room, that she would lock the door behind her and suddenly feel the familiar pangs of loneliness and longing. At moments like these, physically exhausted to the point of collapse, she'd miss him desperately again, and seizing her pen she would pour out her feelings to him: 'Dearest Senechka, I love you so much still! Why did you abandon me? I'm lonely and miserable and afraid without you – don't you know that? Why did you have to go away when you could have stayed with me? We could have been just friends – you could still have cared more for her than you cared for me, given her everything, your tenderness and your caresses, but couldn't you have kept just a little warmth in your heart for me . . .?'

Natasha never sent these letters, but it gave her some relief to pour out her feelings to him once in a while . She just had to let off steam sometimes. While she was writing them, she'd manage to convince herself that it was only external factors that prevented him from being with her: if they were in the same town, if they hadn't parted for ever, she would tell herself, of course he would give her the warmth, understanding and sympathy she needed from him. At these times Natasha would forget the reality of their relationship, the number of times when, even with him beside her, she'd felt so dreadfully alone and unloved. She would forget too what she knew in less troubled times to be true: that she must take responsibility for her own life, that she must be able to stand alone and be strong.

She would forget the strain she so often felt when she was with him, a strain so exhausting that she would often breathe a secret sigh of relief when he'd gone and she could return, unhindered, to her own thoughts and moods. All these things Natasha would forget, and she'd feel only how poignantly sad and isolated her life was without him.

'I feel just like a widow,' she'd written once. 'I wander around all the places we used to visit together when we were still friends – all those places where we used to work together, where we felt so much together. Do you remember those days, when we seemed like one person, with one heart, one mind? Do you remember how strangely close we felt to one another the moment we met, and how that closeness grew gradually into passion? Now I often regret that it did, for it spelt the end of our friendship. Oh, how happy we were before that – our friendship had wings! If we'd stayed friends you'd never have left me, Senya . . . '

But then there'd be times when she could hardly believe there had ever been any intimacy between them, moments of overwhelming misery when an endless series of buried insults would surface and haunt her. At such times all their past happiness seemed nothing but a fraud. She tormented herself with questions she couldn't answer: 'Did he ever love me? If so, does love mean the same thing to him as it does to me? If he did love me, how could he have rejected me like that? How could he not have *seen* how much he was hurting me.... No, I don't believe there ever was any *real* understanding or affinity between us – that famous closeness of ours was just something I invented, something quite artificial and unreal. I wanted it to be true so I thought I could make it true. And to think of the energy and time I've wasted on something completely unreal.'

And she would grow beside herself with rage, recalling bitterly how her work for the Party had suffered in the years she'd been with him. She thought of all the times she'd delegated important matters to other people so as to be free for him, all the times she'd missed crucial meetings, all the times she'd been late. It was hardly surprising that her former reputation as an efficient Party worker had suffered over the years. More than once the comrades had occasion to rebuke her for her slipshod conduct. She blamed him, retrospectively, for the accumulated bitterness and rage she felt at such times ...

* II *

There, in the small room in which she lived alone, amongst the piles of books and papers, was his photograph. It was an old one, one that he'd given her soon after they first met at a literary dinner-party. Although she'd always been one of his supporters and had written a series of pamphlets to popularise his theories, they'd hitherto known each other only by name.

She had arrived at the party with a man she was very close to at that time. 'Guess who's here today,' he said shortly after they got there. 'It's your beloved Semyon Semyonovich.'

Her face lit up. 'Really? Oh do point him out to me, please! I'd so like to meet him!' She was childlike in her excitement.

'What's all the fuss? I fear you'll be sadly disappointed when you do see him; he's not much to look at, and I shouldn't like to think what he's like as a man.' Her friend was clearly nettled and trying to cool her enthusiasm, but Natasha merely shrugged her shoulders in exasperation.

'Oh how stupid you are, talking about him like that!'

'Well, if you're really so keen to meet him, I'll introduce you.' And he went off, leaving her behind. She was smiling, and trembling a little too, for she was pleased and also suddenly nervous of seeing someone she'd thought so much about, in the flesh, perhaps even getting to know him. She saw how he winced when her friend dragged him off to meet her, and the funny eccentric way he behaved endeared him to her at once; Semyon Semyonovich, of all people, was shy! After that she always thought of him as a charmer, a clumsy, comical child of a man who for some reason she found irresistibly touching. She loved to remember that time when they had first met, and the two weeks in that spring when their friendship began and quickly deepened.

The air they breathed was so sweet, so charged with the promise of new unexplored joys – oh, in those days she hadn't known the meaning of loneliness! She overflowed with a new vitality, discovered within herself new strengths, overcame every obstacle in her life and work – in short she came to believe in herself. Of course there'd been the odd anxious moment too, and times when she was actually unhappy and frustrated, but the two of them were so exuberant when they were together that she felt quite cushioned against life's difficulties. Seeing him enhanced everything she did and made her feel irrepressibly happy in those two wonderful weeks. It was as if nothing could frighten or daunt her. Her whole life lay before her and she saw herself boldly striding up a steep mountain path which beckoned her to go up, higher and higher.

'How *can* you live such a solitary life?' her friends (most of them women) asked in amazement. (This was after, uncharacteristically abruptly, she'd broken off all contact, with the other man. 'Don't you feel the need for some sort of family life – or at least some person you're close to, somebody to live with and keep you company?'

She always laughed by way of answer. No, she'd say, she didn't feel at all sad to be living alone – far from it: she was happy to be a single woman again, delighted that her wings were no longer tied and that she was free. She had her work, she had a full life, she needed nothing more. Yes, she assured these friends, she had an extraordinary life, a wonderful life. She was surrounded by close friends and people she loved – she couldn't really imagine what people meant when they talked of her 'living alone'.

What her friends didn't realise was that when she talked of the people she loved she was in fact thinking of him. And since his family – his wife Anyuta and his children – were an inseperable part of him, she loved them too. She wasn't too bothered by Anyuta's somewhat irritatingly conventional 'femininity', or her lack of any understanding of Natasha's life as a single woman. For even though Anyuta's petty bourgeois pronouncements occasionally grated on Natasha's ears, she was, with all her faults, a kind and generous woman who always greeted Natasha warmly. She adored her husband too, worshipped the ground he walked on – that too she had in common with Natasha. And of course he was so brilliant, so good, so loving – how could anyone fail to love him?

Anyuta often teased Natasha when they first met, and she loved to show off what a wonderful family life they had. 'Really my dear, I can't help feeling sorry for you,' she'd say, 'all alone, with no husband and nobody to support you through life. Of course, not every woman is lucky enough to get a husband like my Senya, I'll grant you, and of course marriage isn't roses and smiles all the way. But still, when you've lived with someone for twelve years – and I'll tell you something, my Senya and I have been together all that time and can you imagine, we still behave as though we're on our honeymoon! – then I really feel sorry for you unmarried women. I think it must be wretched to be all on your own all the time, with nobody to care for you and nobody to look after. Just think, dear, Senya is still in love with me! You don't believe me? Well listen to this: I know people don't usually mention such things, but I know what a liberated soul you are ... ' And some intimate detail of Semyon Semyonovich's marital behaviour would follow, to prove to Natasha how much in love with his wife he was.

These intimate revelations always embarrassed Natasha acutely, and she would cut them short. She felt a sense of revulsion and anger, not only with Anyuta but with Semyon Semyonovich himself, and the sickening image of a 'good husband' would obscure for a while the intelligent face of the friend she so loved. She'd wait a while and try to forget Anyuta's anecdotes before visiting their house again; sometimes it seemed to her that these things were said only to exasperate her – sometimes she even imagined Anyuta must be making them all up.

But these irritations were never any more serious than pinpricks on the surface of her life, and could always be soothed away by the joy of their developing intimacy. This intimacy, born of shared political work, opened up a new world to them; it illuminated the hours Natasha spent alone in her little room, it transformed her life.

Then passion came, sweeping them off their feet with a suddenness that took their breath away. Natasha lost her head completely and fell deeply in love.

Before this, she had always been considered 'experienced' in affairs of the heart, and liked to believe that time had taught her good sense. Laughingly she would assure herself that she would never again get passionately involved – she'd suffered enough. She no longer wanted the crises, the traumas, the struggles, the sufferings and misunderstandings of love, she wanted friendship and understanding instead. She wanted the responsibility and commitment of political work, and she wanted to collaborate with people she trusted on something important. That, at any rate, was what Natasha *thought* she wanted – until life decided otherwise for her.

* III *

They'd arranged to travel together to a political meeting in another town, and got as far as buying two tickets for a crowded third-class compartment a few days before when Anyuta suddenly started pleading with him not to leave her. She produced one reason after another why he should stay, and Semyon Semyonovich was beginning to waver. The day before they were due to leave Natasha rushed round to their house to find out whether or not he would be going and found him still undecided.

'I know I really should go,' he said; 'If I don't, they'll certainly find some way of exploiting the situation and knocking our resolution on the head.' ('They' were the opposing faction.) 'But then I don't see how I possibly can. Vityusha's running a high fever, Anyuta's rushed off her feet as it is – in all conscience, I couldn't just leave her here to cope on her own. I know, look, why don't you pop in here tomorrow morning before the train leaves – it's on your way to the station after all – and then we'll see what can be done?'

So the next day Natasha had called round (his house wasn't on her way to the station) only to be met by a sour look from Anyuta and a guilty glance from a harassed-looking Semyon Semyonovich. He couldn't possibly go, he said; but he urged Natasha that it was of the utmost importance that she should attend the meeting. 'I know if I don't go there'll be all hell to pay. If they do defeat our resolution – and they almost certainly will – I'll never forgive myself. But Vitenka has a fever and poor Anyuta's at her wits' end. It's absolutely maddening and I really don't see why I should be made to miss important meetings like this ... '

'Well, it's no great tragedy, we'll try to manage without you somehow and put up a fight – we'll defend that resolution of ours, you'll see' Natasha had consoled him, little suspecting the true cause of his agitation.

So she left on her own for the station. Secretly she couldn't help feeling rather relieved, for now she could consider calmly all the points contained in their resolution, and draw up a series of arguments in its defence. It was a bitterly cold day, and to keep herself warm Natasha paced up and down the frosty platform, her hands deep in her muff, her head full of ideas. She was in a cheerful mood, elated by the prospect of fighting to win and then returning to him with the good news.

'Natalya Alexandrovna, Natalya Alexandrovna!' She swung round. 'It's me: Here I am – I made it!' Semyon Semyonovich stood there, breathless and triumphant. 'Well,

I made my escape – what a time I've had of it! It's a pity about Anyuta, of course, but . . . ' Then the train drew in and interrupted him, and with a familiarity, and a confidence in his rights that seemed to her entirely natural, he took her arm. Their compartment was crowded and they had to sit very close. Time and again their eyes met, and there was something so searching, so unambiguously sexual about the way he gazed at her from behind his gold-rimmed spectacles, that Natasha grew agitated. When his hand brushed against hers as though by accident, she felt it tremble, and soon he'd communicated his agitation to her. Talking became impossible. They spoke only with their eyes, now seeking, now avoiding one another. She felt the current that passed between them and through her, the sweet, tormenting current of desire. The train drew in to a large station.

They got off for a breath of air: the cold air hit them, fresh and aromatic. The great grimy city was far away. They both sighed with relief, as though awakened from some weird and beautiful dream, and gulping down great lungfuls of air, they began to chatter and laugh again. 'Oh how beautiful it is here! Look, hoar frost – Ah, what wonderful air . . . !' They felt so easy together now, their friendship seemed so good, so uncomplicated.

Neither of them felt like returning to their compartment, but as the train was about to move off they reluctantly got in again – and once again Cupid took aim. The train was even hotter and stuffier than before, and they were sitting very close together when Semyon Semyonovich reached for Natasha's hand. This time she did not take it away.

Inarticulately, incoherently, his voice breaking with emotion, he started to tell her about Anyuta and how jealous and unhappy she was. It was quite clear to her that by talking about Anyuta he was actually trying to talk about his love for Natasha. For Anyuta, he said, he'd never felt anything but sympathy and pity. He'd married her because she needed him so much, and now, having lived with her for twelve years, he felt totally estranged from her. He was more and more locked up in his own thoughts and had become increasingly solitary. That was before he met Natasha – for when she came into his life she'd changed everything. Now he'd forgotten what loneliness was. Every day was bright and happy now, for Natasha had unlocked his heart. He needed her. His love for her was like nothing he'd ever experienced before, surpassing all limits of joy and pain. He'd been in love with her for a very, very long time, without ever daring to hope that she might also love him. Falling in love with her had left him as dizzy and helpless as a boy – it was like calf love! And he was terribly jealous too, jealous of the man she'd been close to before meeting him, the man who'd introduced them to each other at the party; he'd been overjoyed when they'd broken off their relationship. He had loved her for years, he said, loved her so hopelessly, so tenderly.

Natasha was stunned. She felt delighted, terrified and extremely confused. Was this her gentle intellectual friend, whose face was now so transformed by passion? No, this was a new Semyon Semyonovich whom she did not know, this man leaning towards her, gazing at her and telling her that he couldn't live without her. This wasn't the dear Semyon Semyonovich she knew, the man with the childish grin. And then what about his family, what about Anyuta and the children? He could never leave them. For a moment a vision of future tragedy flashed across her mind.

'What can we do, Natalya Alexandrovna?' He was in torment, and suddenly she felt overwhelmed by tenderness for him.

'How can you ask?' She addressed him now in the intimate 'you' form. 'I can't think of anything I want more than to be your friend, as if you haven't already given me so much happiness!'

'Oh my darling Natasha.' And oblivious to the staring people sharing their compartment he put his arms around her and kissed her on the forehead. 'Being with you is beautiful: you make me so very happy.'

She gazed back at him. Her lips were smiling but her eyes were filled with tears. 'It's only because I'm so happy,' she whispered, and he clung to her even tighter, murmuring 'My dearest Natasha, my darling.'

When the train finally arrived at their destination they stepped off quite drunk with joy. They were met at the station by friends, who led them off to their hotel, and from there to the first session of the conference. It all went very well. They were both in the best of spirits and enjoyed their evening immensely. It wasn't until much later that night that their friends walked them back to the hotel, and there they took their time to say goodnight. There was more laughing and joking. Natasha loved everyone that night, – even people she usually disagreed with politically seemed wonderfully good and lovable. She felt drunk with happiness and wanted this day never to end so that she could go on laughing with her friends forever. Moments like these never came twice. Today it was all laughter and joy. Tomorrow, well, tomorrow would bring its own problems.

She was right, of course. It was the final day of the conference, and what with all the excitement, the hard work and three nights without sleep, Natasha was beginning to get just a little careless about her secretarial duties. Who could blame her for lacking the stamina to concentrate fully, listen carefully to what was being said, and accurately report everyone's speeches (which, like most speeches at most meetings, were inordinately long). Towards the end of the session the delegates decided that the minutes should be read out. It turned out that Natasha had slipped up in recording the speech of one of the opposing faction, and had somewhat misrepresented his views. All hell broke loose from the opposition; they were convinced that this was some kind of dirty trick intended to discredit them. Natasha was distraught.

And then, as if all this wasn't bad enough, Senya, her beloved Senya, stood up and launched into a fierce tirade against her. The thinking behind it was clear enough to her: he wanted the opposition delegates to think that this was merely some little personal 'dirty trick' of Natasha's, rather than something engineered by their faction as a whole. But she could hardly believe her ears when he suggested that she wasn't really suited to the job.

The meeting ended. A whole crowd of people walked back to the hotel, shouting and arguing, but Natasha was fighting back tears. When at last they were alone together she threw herself into his arms, and, safe at last in his embrace, she burst into tears. Senya would understand, she knew that; there'd be no need to explain. Of *course* he'd be feeling uneasy about what he'd done, betraying her like that, even if it was 'for the good of the cause.' Shouldn't he perhaps have defended her instead, he'd be thinking? She did so want to tell him that she quite understood what he was feeling, but that she understood too that ultimately the interests of their faction outweighed all such personal feelings of the moment. Just as long as he made *some* little gesture to show he was sorry for insulting her pride. She couldn't bear her comrades thinking that a minor mistake, caused only by tiredness, was in fact some awful plot she'd been concocting single-handed.

'You do understand what I'm feeling, don't you, Senya?'

'Of course I do, my poor little love, and I'm sorry. Of course I understand how painful it is for you to have to leave me – but what can be done about it?'

She stopped crying and stared at him, scarcely able to believe her ears.

'And don't you think it's painful for me too?' he continued, gently stroking her head. 'Do you think I feel it any less painfully than you do? But come now dear, it's not as if we're saying goodbye for ever. You must come and see me when we get back – you will, won't you, or else Anyuta might suspect something ... Ah, please don't cry any more my darling. All day I've longed to be alone with you like this. Won't you kiss me, Natasha ... ?'

Was this the right moment to tell him the reason for her tears? How could she explain now, when he had so totally failed to understand anything? He saw she was unhappy, yet he could only imagine that this was because they were about to part. Two large tears coursed down her cheeks and he kissed them away. 'Don't cry now, poor little thing. We *will* see each other again, yes we will, many, many times. ... '

They travelled home in the train with their friends, and when they arrived back they parted formally at the station. They might have been two strangers.

* IV *

Looking back now, she understood rather better why she had cried at the moment of their first parting. At first he had almost persuaded her that it was the sorrow of their separation, but now she knew better – she knew that the cause of her tears was the first affront to her soul and her pride. By now, several years later, many, many humiliations and insults had bothered her, had bruised her poor spirit. And to think it was her Senechka who had done this to her! Didn't he realise that those endless, subtle wounds could break a person's heart? That a damaged heart becomes incapable of love? That her love for him was ebbing away ... ?

In the seven months in which they'd been apart Natasha had been reviewing things, trying to get a clearer perspective on their relationship, and coming gradually to accept that their happiness was now poisoned; nothing remained of all those hours of happiness and the passion of their love-making, nothing, that is, except grief and bitter memories. Senya, she now realised, had failed to hear what she was telling him. She'd stood before him, so vulnerable and eager to offer herself, to give herself to him body and soul – and he had neither seen nor heard her. He'd merely possessed her, as a woman, and then left her feeling even more alone than before, arms outstretched to him. ... He knew nothing about her. He hadn't even *wanted* to know her!

Of course life had dealt him more than his fair share of blows, what with his unbearable domestic life, his constant financial crises and the setbacks he suffered in his extremely demanding work. His family life must be quite intolerable; he lived surrounded by an atmosphere of jealousy and suspicion which suffocated him and hampered his writing. Yes, it was true, his life was one long worry.

'Anyuta very nearly poisoned herself today' – it hadn't been uncommon for their meetings to be prefaced by some such macabre remark – 'and if I hadn't rushed in just in time she'd have been at the morphine. Oh Natasha, what's the answer to this ghastly mess? Tell me what to do ... ' Then he would bury his face in his hands and Natasha would kneel on the floor and stroke his head as tenderly as if he were a sick child she was trying to comfort. His sufferings always moved her.

At first Anyuta's suicide attempts had horrified her, but soon they became such a regular occurrence that she began almost to take them for granted. She certainly never blamed Anyuta, and these acts of frenzied desperation always aroused her deep pity. But it was always for him that she really suffered. *Why* must Anyuta take up so much of his precious time and fill his life with one petty anxiety after another? Why couldn't she see how important his Party work was? Why couldn't she understand that every ounce of his strength had to be devoted to his work? Natasha understood this, of course, which was why she was always so self-effacing, why she never brought her worries to him, why she never told him when she was unhappy, and why he never realised that she too suffered sometimes. All Natasha brought to him was the tenderest love and the greatest admiration for his work; all she wanted was to stand between him and the world, relieve him of his worries, help him bear his cross.

'Ah, how strong you are,' he would sigh sometimes, 'and how unlike Anyuta. You can build your own life and stand alone in the world – she could never survive without me.' And Natasha would smile at him in a motherly sort of way. She could never allow herself to be weak with him, she knew that, for she not only had her problems to cope with but his as well – in fact, she had to bear the entire psychological burden for both of them. She was his support, his consolation, his ray of hope, his one and only joy – yes, she must always bring him joy, for with Anyuta it was nothing but gloom, tears and endless anxieties; with her it must be a perpetual holiday, fun and laughter all the time.

There were times when something would go wrong with this scheme of things, and then she felt revolted by the role she'd chosen to play. Why in God's name did he always have to feel so wretchedly 'sorry' for Anyuta? Could he not feel just a little sorry for *her* once in a while? As if she didn't have enough struggles and worries in *her* life! Sometimes she had vast amounts of highly responsible and very complex work to do, and she'd worry herself sick. Hers wasn't an easy life

– all her other friends in the Party understood this and sympathised, so why couldn't Senya?

'I'm absolutely exhausted today, Senya dear,' she had said once, determined to make him listen to her and see her not merely as his lover but as a woman with a life of her own and problems to deal with. 'I suppose you've heard about this resolution the other lot are putting through – they've been giving me no end of bother about it these last few days and I've no idea what to do.'

'Oh I wouldn't trouble yourself over that,' he had replied. 'It's all really rather trivial – they're trivial people anyway, aren't they? I'd far rather we talked about *us* instead. Lord knows, we've got enough problems. Anyuta's been ill again and the doctor said she must rest, so that means we'll have a get a nanny to live in. But then there's the money problem – you know the state of our finances. Then, oh Natasha, when I see Anyuta wasting away before my eyes, and when I think of everything she's always given me and the children, how she never begrudged us anything, then I feel like a self-centred swine who's good for nothing and no one ... '

When life seemed such purgatory for her lover, Natasha's own problems receded into insignificance and she found it quite impossible to discuss them with him. There were times, although it must be said that these were not very frequent, when it would come home to him quite forcefully that she was always the giver in the relationship, and that he was never anything but the taker.

'I know this is all one long headache for you, Natasha,' he said once. 'I'm an egotistical brute, I know that, and I don't give you half the love you deserve. Sooner or later you'll have had enough. You'll leave me and then I shall go completely to pieces. I treat you so badly. Yet you can't imagine how much I love you and how much you mean to me.'

'But I *do* know, Senechka, indeed I do. Otherwise how

d'you imagine that I could tolerate this situation and continue with it?'

'I'm the best friend you ever had, Natasha my love, I want you to believe that – do you believe me? Sometimes I have the feeling I'm not really getting through to you, you know; sometimes when we're together there's a part of you which I can sense is somewhere far away from me, and then I wonder whether perhaps we're growing apart. You often won't tell me what's on your mind and I find that terribly hurtful. You know how I want us always to share everything – in fact it's more important to me than anything else that we should be close to one another ... '

'Oh Senechka, that makes me very happy; – so it *is* important to you – and I'd thought it was just me who felt like that. Sometimes, you know, I feel I'm not really the sort of woman you need; it's a chilling thought and it terrifies me! But I don't want you to love me just as a *woman*, Senechka. Do you understand what I'm trying to say ... ?'

'Now Natasha, don't be silly ... "

'But yes, you're right, I have felt rather distant from you recently. I don't know why, and I don't want it to be like that; I want us to be able to tell each other everything.'

'Well, why don't you tell me everything then?' He was watching her suspiciously; 'Do you have something in particular you want to tell me? You've been hiding something from me, haven't you?'

'No, not really ... well, yes, I suppose I haven't been completely open with you – and yes, I do have something on my mind which has been worrying me but I haven't felt able to tell you about it.'

'And what is that?'

'You see, although ... Anyway ... Look, you know Anton Ivanovich? He's been visiting me an awful lot recently; he comes to my room and sits and sits, sometimes for hours at a time. And he looks at me in a way I don't like at all – you

51

know, he *eyes* me. I hate it actually, but how can I tell him to get out and slam the door in his face? We have to be able to work together! And then I suppose I *do* feel rather sorry for him too, because I know how lonely he is ... '

'Well Natasha, you really do baffle me sometimes – now I've heard everything! What in God's name has your work got to do with it? And as for pitying this fellow, I'm afraid I find that quite bizarre! He sits there for hours, gazing and sighing – he's obviously hopelessly besotted with you by now – and all you can say is "I feel rather sorry for him .. !" If a man looks at you in a way you find offensive, then just tell him to go and there's an end to it. If, however, you *like* this man pursuing you, then of course that's quite different ...'

'Oh Senechka, don't be so obtuse!' Natasha was angry, but she couldn't help laughing all the same. How could he be jealous! There was only one man in her life and she worshipped him, as he knew quite well, and the most beautiful man in the world would never entice her away from her darling, round-shouldered intellectual Semyon Semyonovich, for no one in the world could compare with him, his wonderful candour and his brilliant, beautiful mind.

Of course his jealousy was quite maddening, but then, as Natasha kept assuring herself, he was naive about a lot of things. Sometimes she could laugh it off, but at other times it outraged and saddened her. There'd been that time when they'd gone to a concert together, for instance, and for some reason he'd got it into his head to be jealous of the violinist. He sulked all the way home, and it wasn't until they'd talked it all over at some length that she finally managed to persuade him that she was a free person and could do as she liked. Then there'd been a similar scene once after she'd had a chat and a laugh with a tram conductor ...

She teased him gently about it, although she had to be careful to choose the right moment. 'What's the matter with you! Do you seriously imagine that I can't look at another man without falling in love with him!'

And of course he'd grin, look abashed, and kiss the tips of her fingers. But Natasha knew that, although she might for the moment have soothed his jealousy, he would never forget that she'd had several lovers before him. For she was a woman with a 'past', and she would always have to answer to him for that. 'You remember you told me you'd been in love with that other fellow, you know, the one with dark eyes? How much did you love him? Did you love him a lot? More than me? Tell me, Natasha!' This was how his interrogations would start.

'But of course I did! Much, much more than you! ... Really, Senechka dear, if I *had* loved him so much how d'you think I could have stopped seeing him so easily? You *know* my feelings for you, and yet you still refuse to accept that it's you I love, Senechka. You're a very clever man, you know, but you can be very silly sometimes.'

'Yes I know, I know that, but I can't help thinking about all those other men of yours and the way they must have wooed and pursued you and said beautiful things to you – *I* could never be like that.'

'But that's precisely what makes me love you, stupid! That's why you're so precious to me and why I find you so attractive – it's because you're not like that.'

'Uh, so you do find me attractive, eh?' he would mumble delightedly, and Natasha would kneel on the floor and enumerate one by one all the qualities in him which made her love him.

Yet his jealousy made her feel resentful and unsure of herself: although she couldn't have said how or why, she felt constantly undermined by him. Even before they were lovers, he'd always been quick to attack the men she'd been in love with before, passionately denouncing this one for making her unhappy, that one for mistrusting her ... Then, when she began to fret and blame herself for her reckless and wasted past, he would have just the right words with which to console her. She would sob hopelessly as she recalled all that she'd suffered from previous lovers, and he would protect her like a true friend.

But it had been a long time since she'd been able to talk so openly to him. In the days before they were lovers, she'd been able to confide in him as she would in a woman friend, and sometimes had even laughingly addressed him as a woman. But her 'Senka', as she called him then, was now a mere echo of the past. After seven months away from him, it seemed to Natasha that there'd been two utterly different people – Semyon Semyonovich, the friend and colleague she's so trusted in those early days, and Senya, her lover.

There was one aspect of their relationship which Natasha only began to make sense of after they'd parted and she'd begun to relive and analyse the past. It was with a sense of amazed outrage that she realised that not only had Senya failed to be sensitive to her feelings, he had actually never recognised her sexual needs as a woman. For all his sensitivity in other matters, his tenderness, his compassion for Anyuta, his natural childlike goodness, which people so often exploited, he could nonetheless be sexually very crude with her. No man had ever insulted her as he had insulted her – even though she realised that he probably did so unintentionally – which was why she knew she ought to forgive him.

Yet the sense of outrage she'd felt during their first night together in the hotel lived on within her, refusing to be forgotten or buried. It was after their friends had left them at the hotel, and they'd gone upstairs to their separate bedrooms. Alone at last, Natasha stood in the middle of her room, her heart racing with joy. He loved her! This man she'd always worshipped actually loved her! Her happiness knew no bounds. She moved about the room slowly, getting undressed and preparing for bed. Suddenly there was a knock at the door – but before she even had time to reply, Semyon Semyonovich had bounded in, locking the door behind him. Natasha stood rooted to the spot, toothbrush in hand and her mouth full of toothpaste.

'How funny you look!' he burst out laughing, 'just like a little boy!' And completely oblivious to her agitation, he seized her in his arms and kissed her. 'You smell of peppermint' he murmured.

'Please wait, let me go, I must rinse out my mouth first . . . ' What could she say? She felt ridiculous but she had a mouth full of toothpaste. She struggled to get away from him, but he was already devouring her toothpaste-smeared lips, her neck and her bare shoulders, smothering her with hungry, insistent kisses – so that her principal memory of that first night they spent together was of the peppermint toothpaste grating on her teeth and the desperate urgency of his embraces. She couldn't respond fully to him for it was all too strange and awkward, too fumbling . . .

Yet afterwards, when he'd fallen asleep exhausted with his head on her shoulder, she felt a new kind of love for him which had quite overwhelmed her, and tenderly, almost humbly, she had lightly brushed his high domed forehead with her lips. It was not just the physical pleasures of lovemaking that she experienced with him, nor the wonderful lassitude which follows passion, but a new feeling of dazzling joy which sometimes quite overwhelmed her; these feelings of reverence, she felt, must be something like pagan people experienced when worshipping *their* idols. But it was not this reverence he wanted from her – he wanted her passionate response, for her to love him as a man; for she was the first woman for whom he had ever felt such passionate desire.

* V *

Sometimes in the long months after they'd said goodbye, Natasha would ask herself whether their love affair had really only brought her suffering and disappointment, whether she wasn't losing sight of the moments of great happiness. For there had been many; there had been breathtaking joy surpassing anything she'd previously experienced.

She remembered the first summer, spent beside a lake in the South of France. There was something almost theatrical about the lush vegetation there; the evenings were hot and sultry. He was living with his family in a house beside the lake and she was staying with her young brother in a hotel up the mountain. At that time they were still observing the 'proprieties' ('for Anyuta's sake', he'd said), and Natasha would regularly visit his family.

That summer it had been just like the times before their love affair began, when it had still been a pleasure to visit his house and feel welcome as a guest. And there, in that rich and fertile countryside, far removed from her work and her commitments at home, Natasha found it perfectly easy to talk to Anyuta.

That summer Natasha and Senya relived the spring-time of their love-affair. They saw a great deal of each other, but invariably in the company of others, which lent a special secret enchantment to their meetings. It intensified their desire for each other and filled each new day with the sweet torment of anticipation. When they met they'd seize moments when nobody was looking to touch hands. Their perpetual closeness aroused desires impossible to fulfil, so instead there were lingering glances more eloquent than words, half-smiles, remarks they alone understood. And then they talked long into the night about politics and their work, and how good *that* was too. They even had political arguments, just like two Party comrades.

She would never forget those nights on the balcony of his house, gazing out at the magical lights of the distant village, the moonbeams dancing in the lake. Oblivious to Anyuta or anyone else coming out on to the balcony, nothing mattered to them now. Everyone else existed outside this private world of theirs. They were aware only of each other and the spell of those burning, semi-tropical summer nights. Settling back in her wicker chair and closing her eyes she felt an overwhelming sense of his closeness to her. She had only to stretch out her hand – but no, she dared not. The more she desired to touch him, the more agitated she would become, and the more she could sense that he too longed to touch her and was leaning towards her ... She would open her eyes and see him secretly smiling at her in the moonlight. And then she'd laugh, with a happiness too great for words. They'd sit up until midnight, talking, arguing, falling silent, talking again – and the joy of those moments, the anticipation of new joys to come, would make her tremble.

At last, stretching, she'd stand up. 'Time for me to go,' she'd say, sighing with sadness and extreme happiness. Leaving him, she'd step inside to say goodnight to everyone. 'We'll see you home!' they'd clamour, and a crowd of people would set off with her to her hotel, up a mountain path which was milky-white in the moonlight. And he'd be there, walking beside her. Every so often she'd brush against his shoulder and these fleeting contacts were as exquisite to her as any caress. When they reached her hotel at last, they would all stand around the wicket-gate saying goodnight to each other, and again he'd press her hand with a special intensity; again those secret eloquent smiles.

She remembered the strains of the popular song 'Hayawatha' and the sounds of laughter which greeted her one evening from the hotel, where the young people danced every night. Through the branches of the trees in the garden she could see the wide open french-windows, and inside, a party in progress. She saw the dancers, their young faces radiant with excitement, flashing past the windows in their bright clothes to the urgent beat of 'Hayawatha', and she saw the sweet childish face of her young brother, all dressed up in his best collar and tie and looking wildly happy. He was in love with a snub-nosed young thing with knowing eyes and hair plaited and tied up in an elaborate bow. She was extremely pretty and she knew it – she knew too that half the boys in the room were after her, but Natasha's brother was too happy to care, for he was in love.

Natasha stood for a long time in the garden below the window, looking in but not wanting to go in, for her heart was too full and she wished only to be alone. The night was so magical that she longed for wings to fly, up to the stars which were calling to her ... Or down, down the mountain path to his house, to fling herself into his arms ... Ah, foolish thoughts! Her desires were as inconsequential as scraps of paper, distracting her and beguiling her so that she could make sense of nothing. She inhaled deeply, drawing in the dense night smell of the tropical flowers. The young couples whirled past the brightly lit windows of the hotel, now merging together, now separating, and the familiar exultant chorus of 'Hayawatha' sounded again and again in her ears.

A brief, vivid summer – distant now as a dream.

Was that the last time – perhaps even the only time – they'd been really happy together? Surely not – why, they'd often been so breathtakingly happy together! Yet she could only frown as she tried to recall the good things, and her frown deepened as she remembered the hours of worry and all the painful things she'd gone through with him. Then she brightened. Yes, there had been a time when it was good!

It was the following spring. She'd rented a room (it had once been a child's nursery) in a large mansion out of town, and there, screened from the world by a dense wall of flowering acacia trees, she had written the last chapters of her most ambitious book, writing feverishly, without a break, to the point of forgetting everything and everyone else. Now she no longer whiled away the hours waiting for his sudden flying visits, for she was completely carried away by her work, and she was working fast too. When a telegram did come from him she was just off to a meeting with a box full of books under her arm, and when he arrived her cheeks were burning and she had that distracted look common to so many writers.

Then she'd been happy! Was it love, or was it the joy of writing? She couldn't have said. At the time it was all so exciting that such questions didn't occur to her. She simply existed in every fibre of her being, living from moment to moment with the pure uncorrupted happiness of childhood. She remembered so vividly those warm spring nights when she'd get out of bed and fling open the windows, and the scent of the acacias wafted into the bedroom, and the moonlight would filter through the foliage on to the table which was still laid with the remains of their supper. It seemed wrong that sleep should intervene and cut short this extraordinary happiness ...

One hot night, shortly before he was due to return, remained particularly clearly in her memory. On that night, half drunk with the sweet scent of the acacias, Natasha felt she'd reached the pinnacle of human aspiration; this happiness was what gave life its meaning. Leaning out of the window, she reached out for a fragrant feathery branch of acacia, picked it and buried her nose in it. 'Mm, how beautiful, how beautiful!' she murmured, laughing and stretching. She longed to wake Senya up, to tell him how much she loved him and how happy she was. Suddenly he woke with a start.

'Natasha, where are you?'

'Here, Senechka darling. It's such a wonderful night, look at these flowers, smell them!' She leaned over him.

'Ah, but that's the smell of you – sweet and sensual': his lips touched her fingers and Natasha felt her heart tremble and soar . . .

No, her love had brought her much more than unremitting misery – how could she have forgotten that exquisite joy, so fragile, so much a world of its own? How could she bear the thought of never seeing him again? . . .

* VI *

Work had been building up over the past weeks to the point where it now required all of Natasha's time and imagination to cope with it. The Party was at a turning point and a great deal was at stake. As always at these times of crisis, Party members worked together especially closely; meetings were charged with new energy and a new spirit of determination, which soon infused Natasha. Her old joie de vivre gradually returned, and she began to enjoy life once more. She felt she was a necessary part of something larger than herself, something she helped to keep alive, and, more important, her friends and colleagues began to treat her with especial warmth, and she knew she was appreciated. Slowly her reserve melted, and now her laughter would often be heard in the dingy little flat they used for secret Party meetings.

'Well, our Natasha Alexandrovna *is* cheerful nowadays,' her friends observed, grinning. 'She must have fallen in love, I suppose,' Vanya, her closest friend, said briskly, not raising his head from her paperwork. 'Well, *are* you in love, Natalya Alexandrovna?'

'Me? In love? Who would *I* be in love with? Surely not you, Vanechka! After all, you're the only man I ever see around here . . . '

'Aha, crafty eh? Shakespeare said it all about women! Now you *have* put me on the spot! But no, Natasha my friend, you really can't fool me, I'm not as blind as you think; I know everything that's going on around here!' Tossing back his long untidy hair, Vanechka glared mockingly at her from behind his glasses. He always made Natasha laugh and she loved to tease him, for she had a specially soft spot for him; she fancied she saw in Vanechka, with his gold-rimmed glasses and his shambling walk, something of Semyon Semyonovich.

It was late and she was exhausted when she finally hurried back home one night. Her back ached, her cheeks burned, her throat was parched, but her mind was at peace, for they'd concluded the first and most difficult part of their work, and she knew things would be easier from now on. She dragged herself up the stairs to her room. All she wanted at that moment was to put on her dressing-gown, and sit down with a cup of hot tea and the latest issue of a magazine which had published a much-discussed article by one of the leading Party theoreticians. It was at times like these, after a long day at work, when she felt thankful to be free, a single woman with the 'moral right', as she put it, to spend her evenings exactly as she liked. Now if Senya was here she'd spend the evening rushing around for him, possibly preparing something for him to eat, possibly arriving home only to dash off immediately to another meeting with him at the other end of town. Tonight it would be just tea and biscuits, a read of her magazine, and then bed. What heaven! And what a blissful, long-forgotten feeling this was, this joy of being alive!

'I don't suppose anyone came for me did they, Darya Ivanova?' she called to the landlady, as she always did, when she passed her room.

'Let me see ... This morning some fellow delivered a book for you, and then later on the telegraph boy came ... '

'With a telegram?'

'Yes, he left it in your room.'

She tried to ignore the sudden stab of anxiety she felt – it was sure to be something to do with work ...

There in her room, lying on her writing desk beside the returned book, was the telegram, and beside it a grey square envelope addressed to her in handwriting which was so familiar to her and yet, at that moment, utterly unexpected and unsettling. Her hands and legs were shaking so badly that she was forced to sit down; her muff slipped off her knees, scattering her purse and all her money and papers over the floor. For a while she stared at the telegram and the letter, incapable of deciding which to open first, then finally she ripped open the telegram: 'Leaving 28th for G'ville. Await you there. Wire me. Will meet you. Semyon.'

The telegram slipped from her shaking hands and her arms dropped helplessly to her sides. On her face was an expression of pure panic. A year ago, this telegram would have made her dance about the room like a young girl, breathless with joy. She would have kissed the telegram and laughed out of sheer happiness. 'Senechka my darling, I'll be seeing you soon ... !' She'd have counted the days until the 28th, and lived only for their reunion.

Now she no longer felt like this – how could she, when for seven months she'd not heard a single word from him? What did he care about her? She might have fallen ill, or died of a broken heart for all he knew. What did he know of her life? He knew nothing of her new political responsibilities and the sacrifices she'd made for her work over the past seven months. He obviously couldn't care less – and yet now, as though nothing had changed, as though he'd forgotten that seven months ago he'd sent her packing, he had the gall to say 'come back Natasha . . . !'

She could visualise him so clearly, and herself beside him. And she had the feeling she'd had so often before – that he was somehow deaf and blind to her, that he only saw her in profile, never head-on as a whole person, as she really was. Yes, that was it, she was a silhouette whose contours he had drawn himself, for that was all he was interested in knowing or seeing of her. And now this telegram – one more stab in the heart, one more insult. No, this time she wouldn't weaken, she wouldn't be caught out. She'd had enough, she told herself, fiercely tossing her head with that proud gesture so characteristic of her, the gesture which had prompted her friends to nickname her 'your highness.'

She reached for her pen. She had to reply, she had to tell him no, a thousand times no. But where was she going to write to him? At his house? Out of the question. Anyuta would have hysterics if she saw the letter. To some address in G'ville? Equally out of the question since he would only be arriving there on the 28th, and if his only reason in going there was to see her, what a blow that would be for poor dear Senechka. He'd break down and cry like a child. No, she'd better discover first of all why he was going to G'ville, and then decide what to do. She snatched up the envelope, tore it open, and began to read.

And as she read, her irritation slowly melted away, her sense of outrage left her, and all the old buried feelings of joy crept up on her. Soon waves of love and an almost maternal

tenderness for her Senechka had washed away all her rage
– for he had never before written to her so lovingly.

He had mourned for her, longed constantly to see her
again, blamed himself a thousand times over. He'd grasped
desperately at any piece of news about her, however trivial,
and in this way had tried to feel that he hadn't completely
lost contact with her. He *knew* about her work and how hard
it was, he *knew* about her various new responsibilities; he
only hoped that all this was keeping her busy enough to take
her mind off him. He only wanted her happiness. As for him,
there wasn't a day when he hadn't longed for her, and now
he could bear it no more. 'My feelings for you are far, far
stronger than anything my reason might tell me,' he wrote,
'and now I can't struggle against my feelings any longer. I
need you.'

His relationship with Anyuta was no better; on the
contrary, he was becoming increasingly irritable with her,
his life at home was hell, and he'd fallen behind with his
work. It was just the other day that this immensely exciting
new theory had occurred to him, which he was very anxious
to tell Natasha about. Wouldn't it be good if they could
discuss it together?

He wanted to follow this idea up properly though, but for
this he badly needed some new material. And so it had
occurred to him that he might visit a certain well-known
professor who lived at G'ville. This professor had offered to
put the entire contents of his library at Senya's disposal, and
he was planning to stay there at least one-and-a-half months,
perhaps two. Now wasn't this a heaven-sent opportunity for
them to meet? She *would* come, wouldn't she? Of course
she'd have to make sure nobody knew where she was going,
or (for Anyuta's sake) with whom, but he knew she was the
soul of discretion in these matters.

There was a PS: as he had no money in the bank, could
she possibly supply the wherewithal for both of them?

Natasha sighed. There was nothing unusual in this request, since it had always been assumed that she was richer than he was – indeed, right from the beginning of their love affair it had been her money that had financed their assignations. She certainly couldn't have been accused of fleecing his family with her expensive tastes!

Senya, like so many bohemians, especially of the Russian intellectual variety, ran his money affairs extremely casually, with the result of course that his family finances were in a state of perpetual crisis. There might occasionally be a little cash in hand but this was never enough to cover the numerous petty debts they accumulated. Natasha, on the other hand, earned an adequate salary from her writing, as well as receiving a small regular allowance from her family. 'I'm just like the man in this relationship,' she used to smile ironically to herself. 'First I ask another man's wife to meet me somewhere, and then I have to bear all the financial responsibility for it ... '

On this occasion, however, she was dismayed by Senya's brisk injunction to supply the cash for their assignation. It was all very well for him to say that, but since she'd just had to subsidise a political campaign with her regular allowance and had only left herself enough for the minimum of her food and rent, her own resources had run very low. How could she possibly get together what was needed? Why, the journey alone would cost heaven knows how much. But she was no longer hesitating about whether or not she would join Senya; that question had been decided for her beyond any doubt as she read his letter. Now the only question was how to surmount all these tedious petty obstacles – in other words, how to get hold of the money.

She began to jot down a few figures – she was no stranger to these sorts of calculations. The train journey would cost at least three hundred rubles, she reckoned, and counting up her cash she discovered that she had just about enough to cover that. But how was she going to lay hands on the rest? She thought at once of the pawnshop. There was her watch – but she'd get nothing but a few sous for that. Then there was her fur collar – but no, that would fetch nothing at all. There was her family, of course, she could write to them – but she rejected this idea immediately: it would be too appalling if instead of sending her the money they merely sent her a reproachful little lecture instead.

'Oh, if only Senya wasn't so peculiar, behaving as though I were some kind of millionaire! I suppose he never wondered *how* I might acquire this vast sum of money – and it's all got to be found so quickly too . . . ' Resentment began to stir in her, and soon she was feeling thoroughly irritable. He never once considered *her* difficulties, particularly when they involved money. He really was a bit of a child . . .

She softened at once. 'Yes, he is a child, which is one reason I love him so much. All intellectuals have this child-like naivety when it comes to practical matters, and that's partly what makes them irresistible. Most of the time he's not living in the real world at all . . . '

Natasha sat up until the small hours doing her sums and trying to get things straight in her mind. But the more she thought, the less she was able to work out a solution. 'How can I possibly *not* go and see him just because of something so stupid as not having enough money? But *where* am I going to find it . . .?' The questions revolved endlessly in her mind and went on tormenting her when she eventually climbed into bed. She lay there tossing and turning sleeplessly all night.

Then new, more serious anxieties began to loom. Her work. How could she possibly delegate all the responsibilities she'd taken upon herself? Part of her knew of course that since it was all running smoothly at the moment it should be quite feasible to find someone to replace her for the three weeks or so she'd be away. She deserved a holiday.

Yet this was easier said than done. And then how would her friends react when she told them she was going off somewhere? She couldn't bear to think of the sarcastic comments and sidelong suggestive glances with which some of them would greet this announcement – that sort of thing would make her miserable for days. There was one particular man – he had rather a bad limp – who'd never liked her. He'd always called her 'Lady Natasha' behind her back, and it was only in the past few weeks that he'd actually begun to treat her with a little more respect. She hated to think what his response would be. He'd certainly take a very dim view of this sudden, mysterious, and evidently clandestine journey, and would consider it – quite rightly, really, – as one more proof of the frivolity he despised in her. 'What did I tell you?' – she could imagine him limping from one end of the office to the other, announcing to the others in that grating voice of his – 'Lady Natasha's nothing but a dilettante!'

But she wasn't going to think about such things any more. She wanted only to set off for G'ville. The very idea of letting Senya down – and herself too – appalled her, for she felt if she didn't meet him this time she would lose him forever. And this time the loss would be irrevocable. 'Oh no, I couldn't bear it,' she groaned, 'not that torture a second time. I'd rather die than face that again   '

The following morning she arrived at the office earlier than usual, looking haggard and distracted, her eyes red from sleeplessness and weeping. Vanechka was there alone, dragging on a cigarette and marking up the daily newspapers with a pencil. 'Hello there, your highness,' he called out to her without raising his eyes. (He was sprawling rather elegantly on a high stool).

'Good morning, Vanechka.' He detected immediately the note of misery in her voice and peered more closely at her over his spectacles.

'What's wrong with you this morning? Feeling blue?'

'Please don't even ask me about it, Vanechka,' Natasha waved her arm helplessly. Life seemed so full of cruel irony and everything seemed so wretchedly wrong that she was over-sensitive even to Vanechka's humorous concern.

'Well, well,' he said in amazement. 'So there *is* something the matter – I'd never have believed it of you. So what are you moping about? Come on, you might as well tell me about it.'

He cleared his papers away as if he meant business, and avoiding her look so as not to embarrass her, he settled himself to listen as solemnly as if this was the confessional. Natasha desperately needed a father confessor, and readily embarked on her long and incoherent story. She had to go away, she told him, 'on family business', but she was being held up by lack of money, yes money, and if she didn't go it would be a terrible disaster . . . 'In a word, it's life or death – yes, someone might die!' she cried and, no longer shy of Vanechka now, she began to sob wretchedly again.

Now Vanechka had seen Natasha preoccupied with her work, and seen her when she was offended and angry, but he'd never seen her weep. He could hardly believe it. Weeping, he felt, was strictly for idiots and children. 'Well, stop blubbering about it!' he shouted as soon as he'd recovered from his amazement. 'Tears won't get you the money. More to the point, tell me how much it is you need. Is it a lot?'

'Yes it is rather, Vanechka, it's three hundred rubles I need.'

'You must be joking – that's a tidy sum, not the sort of amount you'll find lining the pockets of people like us! You must be budgeting for a few luxuries, I'd say, your highness, to want that much cash! I do hope you're not just flinging it around – why you'll be begging on the streets soon if you go on squandering your money like that!'

'Oh but it's not for me, all that money. You see, something just cropped up, Vanechka, something very urgent. Yesterday I got a telegram – you can't imagine how important it is for me to leave, and if I don't lay hands on that wretched three hundred ... Well a person's life is at stake, I can't say more than that – two lives, even.'

'Ah, now I'm beginning to understand; you have to bail someone out, is that it?' Vanechka's face cleared.

'Yes ... in a way, yes.'

'Well, why didn't you say so at once then, instead of inventing some unlikely story about having to visit relatives in Moscow or St Petersburg or wherever, not saying whether it was for a week or for good? Why not just tell me right out that this was some conspiratorial affair which was none of my business, but you needed my help? That would have been fine by me. I wouldn't have asked any questions; I'm not over-inquisitive, you know, and I'm not wet behind the ears either. If you don't want to talk about it I won't ask questions, but I do want to help if I possibly can!'

Natasha didn't dare contradict Vanechka's interpretation of her dilemma, however awkward the deception made her feel, for he was already considering various ways he might get hold of the money for her, and she was terrified that if she even hinted at the truth she might lose his sympathy. Was it such a crime to deceive Vanechka like this? It was only a loan, after all, and Natasha was always as prompt as a Prussian in repaying her debts, everyone knew that. An article of hers was already at the printers; she could let her royalties from that stand surety for the sum ...

'Let's forget these financial transactions for the moment,' said Vanechka, 'and try instead to think who might be sitting on the pot of gold. Now there's that old fellow who's sympathetic to us, you know who I mean – he's got a fair bit of capital. But of course he may not feel like obliging just now.'

'Of course I know who you mean, dear Vanechka, and yes do please try him. It would be much easier for you to ask him than for me. But you can tell him the money's for me and that I'll vouch for it. Look, why don't I write a receipt for you to take to him ... ?'

'But you're nowhere near getting that money, and you're already begging him to take a receipt for it! There's no sense in rushing things, though I can see you've got quite a head for business ... Oh lord, I've been chatting away all this time and I've completely forgotten to make that phone-call. It's all your fault, your highness, you shouldn't distract honest workers from the path of duty.'

Two days later Vanechka triumphantly handed Natasha an envelope. 'Here you are, you're in luck – I did it!'

'Vanechka, you're an absolute dear!' Natasha delightedly leant forward to kiss him, but he stopped her. 'Now steady on there with the kissing and the "Vanechka dears", and take your receipt. He's a tight-fisted old chap, isn't he? Moaned and groaned about times being so hard, and the fact that he'd just given away a lot to someone else and he really needed it for himself. Anyway, I only had to mention that it was you who was vouching for it and that did the trick at once. Then I produced the receipt, and at that the old fellow softened up completely ... Look, why are you tucking that envelope away without even counting the money? You never know, I might have cheated you and taken a hundred for myself.'

'And I wouldn't mind, that's the honest trust!'

'So why did you ask for three hundred if you could have managed with two? Or are you planning to splash out that third hundred on a new fur coat? You should be ashamed of yourself, your highness. Strikes me there's something suspicious going on here. Who is this person you're bailing out, I'd like to know? Unless, of course, you're really slipping off to a sophisticated christening party or something, in which case you can certainly count me out as a friend of yours!'

Natasha laughed and squeezed his hand. 'I don't know how to thank you enough, dear Vanechka; you've saved my life. From now on I shall always think of you as my guardian angel.'

'Hah, and I suppose you'll make the sign of the cross and bow down before me when we meet?'

'Now don't be stupid, Vanechka.'

'Well what *I* think is really stupid,' Vanechka retorted, pausing in the doorway, 'is to call someone your guardian angel. Just think what you're saying! If you're really so grateful to me why not send a postcard from wherever it is you're going to. I'd be very interested to hear from you.' Natasha blushed. 'All right, all right,' he said quickly, sensing her embarrassment, 'I won't give you away, cross my heart. When I get your card I won't tell a soul where it was posted from – I'll carry the secret with me to the grave. It's just that I'd like to hear from you, that's all. If you really trust me you'll write to me, and if you don't I'll know our friendship isn't up to much.' Looking at her sternly, Vanechka pulled his fur cap over his ears, and disappeared through the door.

* VII *

The journey to G'ville seemed endless and by evening, after several hours in the train, Natasha was almost beside herself with nervousness, one moment in a frenzy of joy, the next full of gloomy apprehension. Over and over again she imagined their meeting and felt supremely happy, but then the thought of the intervening hours on the train dampened her high spirits and soon anticipation had turned to anxiety. What if he didn't meet her at the station? And even if he did, what if she missed him on the crowded platform? If he didn't meet her she'd have to wait for him until morning, and pass an endless night in some unfamiliar hotel – and that would be unendurable ...

At last the train slowed down and she could see the bright lights of G'ville station through the window. Natasha's heart was thumping so wildly that she was convinced her fellow-passengers could hear it. She was frozen to her seat in a fever of anxiety, and there she sat, shaking and overcome, unable to make her numb, trembling fingers get the window open. When at last she did, she leant out, her body tense. Was he there? 'Oh lord, please make him be there; please make him meet me,' Natasha whispered, for although naturally she didn't put any faith in prayer, it did ease her mind a little to repeat the familiar childhood words. How crowded the platform was, what a lot of people! However would he see her ... ? Then, yes, it was him! Yes, she was sure of it! Her legs nearly gave way under her and her heart thumped even louder. But now it was for joy – everything was going to be all right!

For hours Natasha had sat in that train picturing the moment when she and Senya would meet. She had imagined them rushing towards one another, oblivious to the crowds and fear of being recognised; she had imagined them falling into each other's arms, kissing and embracing; she had imagined tears of joy ... But things didn't happen quite like that.

Jumping on to the platform, she stumbled and fell, dropping her umbrella and handbag. She bent to gather up her scattered possessions. The next thing she knew Senya was beside her, and before even greeting her he'd stooped down to pick up her umbrella. It was only then that he stretched out his hand to her, by which time Natasha was so distraught that she could only shake it, silently, as she might do with a complete stranger. 'Let's be off then, Natasha. I'm afraid there are a lot of people here – we don't want to bump into someone we know, do we? I think I'd better walk ahead to the hotel; you just follow me.' So saying, Senya walked away, stepping out briskly along the platform towards the exit and looking for all the world as though he had nothing at all to do with her.

Half-stunned, and still hardly able to grasp that the long-imagined reunion had taken such a bizarre turn, Natasha trailed behind him, trying not to lose him from sight altogether. As it was, she managed to get only fleeting glimpses of him, and then he seemed strangely different – maybe it was just that he'd put on weight, or his beard had grown. He'd always had this fear that they might bump into an old acquaintance when they were out together, that was nothing new to her. (She vividly remembered being with him in a remote little town where it was inconceivable that they would meet anyone who might know them, but where he had nevertheless insisted that they follow each other in this strange Indian file.) But today Natasha found Senya's persecution mania utterly exasperating. 'Why, he didn't even say hello properly!' she fumed. 'And after all those months! He could have said just one word, or asked me just one question about myself ... '

They crossed a broad deserted square lit by flickering lamps and she followed him as he made for a hotel, a very ordinary sort of a place with a doorman in braided uniform standing outside. Inside, a messenger-boy with shiny buttons took her bags and led them into the lift. And here at last Semyon Semyonovich moved towards her and reached for her hand. 'Well, what d'you think of it?' he murmured. Natasha, with an instinct born of habitual discretion, drew back and indicated the messenger-boy

beside them. 'Oh don't you worry about that!' Senya
laughed. 'I told them I was waiting for my wife, you see, so
I've booked us into a double room. We can move to another
hotel later, but this one'll do nicely for the time being, I
think. You see how experienced I'm getting at all this!' He
grinned slyly at her over the tops of his spectacles, and
Natasha smiled back; but it was a small unhappy smile. On
her way to meet him her cheeks had been flushed, and she'd
radiated such joy that the other passengers couldn't help but
look at her. Now the fire in her eyes had gone and she felt
confused, bewildered and tired. This wasn't the Senya she
knew – this man in the lift beside her seemed like somebody
else, somebody she'd never met before.

The boy with the buttons led them out of the lift and along
the corridor to their room. He flung the door open to reveal
a bare, anonymous, rather shabby double room, indistinguishable from any hotel room anywhere in the world.
Leaving them standing there, he went back for their bags;
then, after taking his time bidding his guests goodnight, he
finally took his leave of them.

Senya was in an exceptionally lively mood. He'd been so
longing to see her, he said, he was so excited and happy. 'But
now let's have a good look at you – why, you *are* thin! Or
is it just that you're tired from the journey?' He put his arms
around her. She was standing facing him with her arms
thrown back, struggling to remove her hat; a pin was caught
in her veil and she could not get it out. 'Let me go a moment,
Senechka dear,' she said. 'I must take off my hat.' But Senya
merely clasped her to him even tighter. 'My darling
Natasha,' he whispered, kissing her; 'How I love you, how
I've longed to see you – I've wanted you so . . . '

By this time Natasha had abandoned the struggle to
remove her hat and was lying across the double bed. She felt
awkward and uncomfortable. Lying there underneath him,
his hot breath burning her face, her hat dragging at her hair

and the pins digging into her scalp, she suddenly felt once more, and quite terrifyingly, that he was a complete stranger to her. That unique and powerful joy which had given wings to her journey here broken into a thousand pieces, crushed by Senya's rough and brutally hasty embraces.

'Kiss me, Natasha, don't turn away from me. Don't you love me any more, dear?' She couldn't speak. Her only response was to clasp his dear head and smile at him. There were tears in her eyes. For all he knew they were tears of happiness, but she was past caring what he thought now. She knew that she was crying from the depths of her soul, crying for one more dream destroyed, one more irreperable insult, one more wound to her tired heart.

Later that night while he slept, exhausted and at peace, Natasha sat up beside him in the bed, gazing into the darkness and trying to make some sense of her feelings. 'I suppose in his own funny way he does love someone – although that someone is certainly not me. Maybe he loves Anyuta, or maybe he just loves things as he would like them to be, rather than as they really are. And to think it was for him that I left work, ran into massive debts, rushed here, there and everywhere organising this trip, one moment out of my mind with joy, the next moment worried sick about the whole thing – to think it was he who gave me something to live for, and believe in, and look forward to ... What a fool I've been, what a fool ... !'

Senya's embraces that night had been uncontrollable, violent – how could she ever have thought of him as a real friend when he so evidently had no sensitivity towards her at all, and when his interest in her was obviously so crudely sexual? Why had she come? Waves of despair swept over her, and she was overwhelmed by a sense of hopelessness so boundless that she could do nothing but sob. She'd never felt so alone at home, thousands of miles from him, as she did

75

now, sitting in the bed beside him, violated, abandoned, desperate. At home she could at least dream and hope; here her dreams had been irretrievably shattered.

Natasha got up next morning with a strange sense of apathy, her feelings numb. Senya, on the other hand, was obviously in the best of spirits. 'Well now, Natasha, do tell me everything you've been doing since we last saw one another,' he said as they sat drinking their morning coffee beside the unmade bed which made their shabby hotel room seem particularly horrible to Natasha. 'Come on, tell me who you've been seeing and all the latest news about our comrades.' But at that moment Natasha had no desire to tell him anything ever again. Yesterday – ah yesterday! – with the train steaming into G'ville, she'd imagined herself telling him all her news, an endless succession of stories about what she'd been doing. She'd pictured them both so clearly, talking the night away until dawn – she'd even tried conscientiously to recall all the particularly important details of her life for him. She'd decided, too, to confess all her misgivings about their relationship, to try and express some of the resentment she felt for him. Then (for he would of course be very upset by her criticisms) she would stroke his head to show him she forgave him and understood him, and slowly the old harmony between them would be re-established.

And only when words were no longer adequate would they discover the ultimate expression of their feelings in sexual passion, that bright burning force which was so very beautiful, which encompassed the colours of her dreams.

But now, after that soulless reunion at the station and their banal night of love together, Natasha had no desire to tell him anything, and her responses were so listless and reluctant that he began to look anxious. 'My dear, you don't appear to be in very good spirits today,' he ventured at last, peering into her face.

'I just didn't get enough sleep, that's all. I'm worn out.'

'You poor thing – one night in bed together and I've worn you out. What are we going to do with you, eh?' He laughed, evidently very pleased with himself, and reached out for the slice of bread and honey which Natasha had prepared for him. She raised her eyebrows with displeasure, and was just about to deliver herself of some uncharacteristically snappish remark when there was a knock at the door.

'Who's there?' called Senya, hurrying to open it. It was a telegram, addressed to the town's poste restante and redirected to the hotel, and it was from Anyuta. Kokochka had the measles; Anyuta was at her wits' end, rushed off her feet. 'So this is it,' said Senya with a sigh that seemed to fill the entire room. To Natasha he looked as vulnerable as a child, standing there dismayed with his head bowed, his legs planted wide apart. Suddenly something changed within her: all her old tender feelings welled up inside her and washed over the pain and anger of the past hours. Yes, now at last she could see before her the man she'd always loved – and still did love – her poor troubled Senya whom she found so touching, so vulnerable.

Natasha leapt up from her chair to his side, clasping his head and kissing him again and again, as though she had only this moment seen him and recognised him. 'Why Natashechka dear ... ' he murmured, confused by such sudden, tempestuous tenderness. 'Look, hold on a moment, there that's better. Now first of all we've got to decide how on earth to sort this wretched business out – oh lord, what's to be done about Anyuta and Koko?' He flung out his arms in a gesture of helplessness, and Natasha caught his hands in hers, covering them with kisses and murmuring inarticulately as she did so; 'Oh my darling Senya, d'you know I feel as if I'd only just come, only just recognised you after so long,

so long without you? Oh Senya, the whole world looks to you
for advice and then a little thing like this happens and you
are so defeated! Oh, I thought I had lost you forever, and
you mean everything to me, Senya. Oh, how happy I am to
have found you again ... '

* VIII *

Since Senya felt it would be awkward to hide out any longer
in their first hotel they moved the next day to another, a
large, genteel, formal place. Natasha arrived first, announced herself under a false name and was shown two
rooms a respectable distance from one another along the
same corridor. She selected the brighter, more spacious
room for Senya, since he had to work, and took for herself
the other, a little dog-kennel of a room; but while waiting for
him to arrive she shifted the sofa, arranged her books and
ran out for some flowers, so that her kennel was soon almost
habitable.

He entered her room unexpectedly – he never knocked,
always burst in like this – while Natasha was sitting at her
desk writing the postcard she'd promised to send Vanechka.
'Ah, here you are,' he said, 'I've had such a job finding you.
They've mixed up all these damned room numbers, so that
57 comes after 85, and I've been traipsing up and down the
corridor – never mind. You *have* made it nice and
comfortable in here, you clever thing ... God, I'm exhausted, I had to take a long walk around the town to kill
time before coming here,' he sprawled out comfortably on
the sofa, 'and I've not had a moment to sit down. Now what

time is it? Aha, six already, well, time for me to go off to the professor's.'

'What, today? Surely that can wait till tomorrow?'

'No no, I'm afraid it can't. You see, Anyuta may have written to tell them I left home on the twenty-eighth.

'Well, what if she did? Why can't you simply tell her the truth, that you didn't visit the professor straight away? There's no earthly reason why she should leap to the conclusion that you're here with me – as far as she's concerned I'm completely out of your life now.'

'Ah, but that's not the point, is it? You *know* what Anyuta's like – if I don't go I shall be constantly worrying lest something of all this reaches her. No, whether you like it or not, my dear, I'm going to have to show my face there today.' It was useless to argue. Natasha felt that his determination to keep Anyuta in ignorance virtually amounted to mania, but she refrained from saying so.

'So what have you been up to while I've been out?' he asked. 'Writing?'

'That's right.'

'A letter, eh?'

Now Natasha knew she wasn't supposed to mail letters directly from G'ville – she was under strict orders not to – but was meant instead to send them by a circuitous route via a woman friend of hers who acted as an intermediary. She felt acutely embarrassed, for the postcard lying on her table addressed to Vanechka bore not only a view of G'ville but a message in her own hand which made some reference to the town.

'So who are you writing to?' Natasha was by now very flustered, and this provoked Senya to lean across the table, trying to spy out the address on the card. Natasha tried to conceal her embarrassment with a little laugh, and covered up the card with both hands. 'I'm not telling you and I'm not showing you – it's my secret and there's an end to it.'

79

'Well, if it's a secret we'll soon get it out of you – now give me that card at once! You won't? Being difficult, eh? So you're going to make me take it by force, are you?' They started to struggle – playfully at first, for both were equally anxious to make it seem a game. But there was nothing playful about the grim expression on their faces.

'What's happening, Natasha? This is something quite new, you've never hidden letters from me before.'

'But why shouldn't I, if I don't want you reading my letters? It's none of your business who I write to ... Let *go* of me – how *dare* you be so violent with me ... ?'

He finally managed roughly to part her fingers and painfully wrenched the postcard out of her hands.

'Don't you dare read that! This is despicable of you!' Natasha screamed at him in a rare fit of fury, and in a flash she had snatched it from him, torn it into tiny pieces and thown them into the waste-paper basket under her table.

'Natasha!'

They glared at each other like two sworn enemies waiting to attack. Natasha was breathless, her cheeks burned with rage. 'I despise you – how dare you attack me like that, how dare you be so violent ... ? You have no right to read my letters ... ' Her trembling lips kept repeating the same words over and over again: 'Despicable ... attacking me ... how dare you ... ?'

'Oh Natasha, Natasha, what are you saying? So it *is* true then!' groaned Senya, covering his face with his hands and collapsing on to the sofa. He'd never failed to melt Natasha's heart when he looked so pitifully helpless, but now she was too baffled to feel any pity for him: 'Can *what* be true? What *are* you talking about?'

'No, you don't need to tell me – you've found someone else, some other man you've fallen passionately in love with, I know ... '

'You know nothing of the sort – you've taken leave of your senses, Senya! Whatever gave you such a ridiculous idea?'

'Well, I didn't want to tell you this but recently I received two anonymous letters with various details about you and some man ... '

'Which you believed – well, now I've heard everything!'

'No I didn't believe them, in fact I burnt them right away and put them out of my mind; but now, well I'm not so sure. I really don't know what to make of your behaviour just now, Natasha, confused and embarrassed, stubborn and then suddenly losing your temper with me like that – you've never spoken to me in that way before – so that's why I felt it might be true that you'd been seeing another man ... Oh no, I couldn't bear it ... Why did you come, in that case, and why have you been deceiving me all along? The least you can do now is to tell me the truth, and stop driving me out of my mind.'

'So you think I'm lying to you, do you! Look Senya, I haven't any idea what you're talking about, but I only wish you could hear yourself sometimes so that you'd realise how foolish you sound when you go on like that. What possible reason do you imagine I'd have for deceiving you? What would be the point of saying things I didn't mean? Why should I want to do such a thing to you? Tell me that!'

'Pity perhaps, I don't know ... '

'Pity? For you?'

'Yes – you're such a good person Natasha, so generous ...' such deep lines of grief had etched themselves on his face, and he seemed weighed down by such suffering that before she knew what she was doing she had knelt down on the floor beside him and was kissing his hands. 'Dearest Senya, why do you think all these foolish things and make yourself suffer so? How can I make you understand that it's *you* I love, and that *you're* the only man I could ever possibly want?' She clung to him.

He resisted her kisses half-heartedly, still fearful that by responding he might be condoning some frightful deception of hers. 'So what about that letter then?' he muttered, his eyes still smouldering with suspicion.

'You won't give up will you, stupid! Look, if you're really that bothered about it, why not just take it out of the waste-paper basket and read it – go on, read it!' She ran to the table, dragged out the basket from beneath it, tipped it upside down and shook it. Fragments of postcard fluttered to the floor, and while they both squatted down on their heels to piece them together Natasha quickly told Senya about her financial negotiations and about Vanechka's invaluable help. Senya knew Vanechka, of course – knew too that he couldn't possibly be a rival for Natasha's love – and the jocular contents of her card to him soon put paid to all his suspicions.

'But you frightened me badly, Natasha dear, making such a ludicrous performance out of the whole business,' he still sounded quite vexed with her. 'What got into you?'

'I suppose I was afraid you'd be angry with me for writing from here. But then I felt I *had* to write to Vanechka since he asked me to, and since he did do both of us such an enormous favour. I know Vanechka – I know he'd rather die than give away a secret.'

'Yes, I see all that now, of course. But I do think it would be extremely imprudent of you to write to anyone from here. What if that card had been accidentally intercepted and someone else got their hands on it before Vanechka? And what does *he* think you're up to anyway?'

'Who cares? It doesn't bother me a bit: I suppose he must realise I'm involved in some great romance, and I expect he'd like to know who the man is too – but he also knows quite well that it's none of his business.'

'I wouldn't be so sure. You see he's bound to put two and two together, see some coincidence here, make some connection there – sooner or later he'll discover that I've been to G'ville too, and before we know it there'll be a lot of unpleasant rumours and speculations flying around ... ' His tone was becoming more and more peremptory. 'No, you can do whatever you like when you're at home, but please, I do beg of you, don't on any account write to anyone from here, not even your dear friend Vanechka.'

'Well if you find the whole idea of my writing to people so unpleasant, then of course I won't,' she replied drily.

He regarded her closely. 'Still sulking, eh Natasha? Upset about being ordered around?' He hugged her. 'What's to become of you women, tell me that – getting into trouble all the time! All right, I admit at first I didn't understand what was going on, but now I see it all ... ' Natasha tossed her head in that defiant gesture of hers he knew so well. 'Ah now, don't be annoyed with me. Come now dear, I was only joking. Now that terrible burden of worry is off me I feel so happy and I'm not angry with you at all any more, so do let's be friends again. Oh darling, you can't imagine how terrified I was – I thought I was going to lose you, and if I had ... Well I don't think I could live without you.' He put his arms around her and clasped her head to his chest. 'I've never been so happy as I am with you, Natasha; I could stay with you forever and never think of the time ... Oh my god!' He jumped up, clasping his head. 'The professor – I completely forgot about him! It's seven o'clock already. I must leave you at once, Natasha, and run – goodbye darling, see you later ....!' He was out of the door in a flash.

Slowly, deep in thought, Natasha gathered up the scraps of the postcard and threw them once more into the basket. She felt enormously tired. She longed to go home. An anguished thought was taking shape in her mind: they were strangers, complete strangers to one another ...

* IX *

It was much later that evening when Senya returned to the hotel. He entered Natasha's room in an exhilarated mood, bubbling over with the exciting new ideas he'd brought from his discussion with this professor who worked in the same academic field.

'It's absolutely splendid! I've finally met someone I can talk to without talking down or translating everything into simple language – now there's a real intellectual for you, someone who has his own highly original responses to every question, and who forces you to clarify your own position. Of course he made me realise very clearly what a vast number of issues there are to be worked out yet – I shall have to be far more rigorous in my analysis and pursue a great many more questions, but nevertheless it was all tremendously pleasing! Oh you can't imagine how starved I've been of that kind of real intellectual stimulation. I suppose it was only after talking to him that I realised how much I really do need an intelligent friend to discuss some of my ideas with systematically, and generally to encourage me in my work ... '

He chatted on for several minutes in this vein, and was so naively pleased with himself that it never occurred to him that his remarks might be evoking a less than sympathetic response from Natasha. Not for one moment did he realise that every word pierced her like a needle. So apparently she was not the 'intellectual friend' he so badly needed to provide him with 'intellectual stimulation'. So she'd been completely and utterly wrong all these years when she'd imagined she was encouraging him to develop his ideas and actually helping him with his work.

'Might I enquire,' she interrupted caustically, 'what it was the professor said to you that was so amazingly intelligent that he even cast doubts on the correctness of your own position?' She could hardly have been more provocative, yet it made little impression on Senya, who merely replied that he didn't feel up to repeating the discussion for her benefit at that moment, but that he'd gladly do so the next day. But Natasha wasn't going to let him off so lightly, and questioned him closely, persisting with unusual tenacity in eliciting answers from him. He only had to hint that the professor wasn't in total agreement with one of his opinions, and she'd be defending it as if her life depended on it – as if this were the cause of her huge anxiety.

Little did Senya know of Natasha's true feelings. If she'd allowed him a glimpse into her mind just then he would have seen, to his amazement, that for the first time in all the years he'd known her she was jealous. Natasha, who hadn't once been jealous of Anyuta, and even when their love affair was at its most passionate had genuinely shared all his fears over Anyuta's last pregnancy and confinement, yes, Natasha was now suffering the pangs of a blind and tormenting jealousy over some old professor whom she'd never even met. This man, it seemed to her, had quite effortlessly replaced her in Senya's life, making her superfluous precisely in those areas in which she'd always before believed she was so necessary to him.

Senya continued to summarise the professor's arguments for her, but in a bored and careless manner as though they couldn't possibly be of any real interest to Natasha and he was merely repeating them in order to satisfy her idle curiosity. Natasha meanwhile continued to take malicious pleasure in pouncing on every one of the professor's illogicalities and non-sequiturs, pointing them out to him with increasing vehemence. But Senya wouldn't be drawn. 'If you'd assimilated his entire argument you'd understand what I've been saying a little more clearly and you'd realise it's far more complicated than that,' he countered in an airy manner which she found particularly exasperating, and then added insult to injury with a yawn: 'Anyway I'm tired, time to turn in now. Sleep well, Natasha.'

'But you can't go to bed yet – I mean, I thought we'd sit and talk a while longer, I haven't seen you all day ... '

'Talk? But my dear d'you realise it's already way past midnight? No, let's wait till tomorrow, then we can have a really good long chat together. I haven't been sleeping at all well lately, and tomorrow I absolutely must start work first thing because I arranged to visit the library with the professor. I really must get some rest.'

'Yes. *We* must get some rest, mustn't we?' At that moment she found the way he always emphasised his needs and disregarded hers quite intolerable. They kissed perfunc- torily, as she imagined two people long-married must kiss, and Senya turned to walk out of the room, stopping at the door to remark; 'Well Natasha, I do think it was a brilliant idea of mine to come to G'ville – I've had a tremendously pleasant day. Do sleep well, won't you dear, and see you in the morning.' He nodded amiably and closed the door behind him.

Natasha slammed the bolt and slumped down on the bed.

She'd spent an entire day on her own. Hours of loneliness had intensified the doubts and depressions of the previous night – now he'd gone without having begun to talk to her properly, and all he could say as he went off to bed was what a marvellous day he'd had! What an insulting way to treat her, his friend and lover, his companion in work and his comrade in struggle; he'd never behaved with such blatant bad manners before. She'd never forgive him.

She thought back to the days when he *had* listened to her
ideas, and valued them, and of the confidence she'd derived
from knowing this. It was he who'd given her the strength
to overcome all sorts of setbacks and unfriendly criticism at
work, and to soldier on with her political work. He'd
believed in her, he'd valued her intellect and her ideas, and
nothing else had mattered to her. But what if he'd merely
beguiled her into thinking he was taking her seriously, just
because she was 'his woman' and his property. She shivered.
How would he respond if she called him an ugly old fatface,
she wondered; maybe he'd respond to the insult in exactly
the same emotionally detached manner in which he'd
spoken to her today. She felt a new and quite savage rage,
closer to hatred than anger.

'I shall go to him at once, tell him just what I think of him,
tell him everything, and tomorrow I'll go straight back home
to my friends. This is no life here – it's nothing but
aggravation and anxiety and I'm sick of it! And I don't even
love him any more – I hate him . . . ' Natasha strode to the
door. But the moment she turned the handle she paused, as
she pictured herself struggling to explain her feelings to him,
foolishly attempting to elicit his sympathy and understanding . . . With a sense of helpless anger she sank back on to
her bed.

They were divided now by a wall which no words could
break down. Indeed, it seemed as if the more they tried to
communicate with each other the more impenetrable it
became, and she knew that any words they might hurl at
each other in uncontrollable rage would stick, deepening this
silence which already cut them off from each other. She was
deluded to imagine she could explain how unhappy and
humiliated he made her feel. Why bother? He wasn't really
listening to her. She might as well keep her mouth shut, bury
her resentment. To hell with it, why should she explain,
when she could quite simply announce, without any fussing

or psychologising, that she had to leave? She could tell him she had urgent work to do, it couldn't be helped, she would just have to go, let him stay with his professor! She would feel miserably lonely, but better that than being perpetually hurt and humiliated.

Natasha began to take off her clothes, pulling irritably at the tapes on her underwear, for all she wanted now was to lie down, sleep, and not have to think about anything. She was exhausted. But the tapes seemed to have their own mindlessly malignant purpose in defeating her, and knotted themselves more tightly as she struggled with them. 'Damn you!' she shouted, for to be mocked by mere objects, after all she had suffered, was more than she could endure. 'I'll just rip you off then!'

She flung off her clothes, leaving them in a crumpled heap on the floor, hurriedly brushed out her long hair and plaited it into two braids which she tied with white ribbons. It was only as she was putting on her dressing gown and was about to get into bed that the sadness welled up afresh inside her. Senya had always loved her with her hair in plaits, and the dressing gown carried all sorts of tender memories; he used to tell her it was more attractive than any of her dresses, and he loved to wrap her up in its soft folds while he embraced her. How could she leave him before he'd even seen her in it? And how could she leave him when she felt so bitterly angry with him? She paced slowly about her little room, absent-mindedly tidying things away.

It seemed so absurd that she should be in her room in this state of turmoil while he was only a few steps away. Wouldn't the natural thing simply be to go in and see him, pour out her grievances and then give him a great big hug, showing that she forgave him for hurting her feelings so badly that day? And if he didn t understand why she was so angry with him, then she must at least *try* to explain, and without losing her temper either. Yes, she *would* try to make him understand her and listen to what she was saying. If she didn't have it out with him there and then she'd never get to sleep that night. What was their love worth, anyway, if they concealed their most important feelings from one another? If she didn't speak to him how would she ever banish this monster of hatred and anger gnawing at her heart?

Gathering the wide folds of her dressing-gown, she opened the door a crack, furtively glanced up and down the corridor to make sure nobody was around, and quickly went out. Her slippered feet sank into the deep pile of the red carpet. The corridor seemed endless. 64, 66, 68 – yes, 68, that was his room, those were his boots outside the door. She hesitated a moment at the door. What if he were asleep? After all it was over an hour since they'd said goodnight. But stronger feelings than these finally impelled her to turn the handle of his door – the longing to see him again and to caress his dear head, the desire to melt the icy rage in her heart and to banish the feelings of uncertainty she'd had all day. The door squeaked as it opened, the light from the corridor shone into Senya's face, and he awoke with a start: 'Who's there? What is it?' Without his glasses he was too short-sighted to recognise her immediately.

'It's me dear, Natasha.' She closed the door softly behind her and went over to his bed where she knelt on the floor beside him.

'Aha, Natasha, fancy you coming in like this!' There was more than a hint of complacency in the way he greeted her which cut her to the quick.

'I've come because I've been feeling very bad, Senya, very bitter and angry and lonely ... '

'Oh I am sorry about that – well, you mustn't let it get you down. Afraid of sleeping alone, are you? Well, don't then! I'm always here, you know. Ah, and I see you've come to seduce me in that lovely gown of yours, you wonderful, fascinating woman . . . ' He put his arms around her, trying to draw her on to the bed beside him. She resisted at first, then responded halfheartedly to his kisses, but at last managed to twist her face away from his. 'Wait a bit Senya, please, not just now. I've got other things on my mind at the moment, which is why I came in to see you. I wanted simply to lie here in your arms for a while and get warm, and then have a little talk.'

'Oh that's all you want, eh? I don't know, you women baffle me sometimes, you really do, with your excuses and justifications. Now it's only this you want, now it's only something else completely . . . You love to look all innocent, as though you'd never had a sinful thought in your life, don't you, as if it were men who were always leading you on. But it was actually you who came to my bedroom and woke me up. Now look at you – one minute it's hugs and kisses, next you're telling me to keep my hands off . . . Ah, now what is it, Natasha darling? Have I hurt your feelings? But I was only joking! I'm *glad* you came, honestly I am. Oh my darling, my own sweet Natasha. Look at you dear, you came in here to get warm and you're sitting there on the floor – your feet must be like ice. Come to me, my love.'

Natasha's abandoned dressing gown gleamed white against the dark hotel carpet.

'Well I don't think there's anything more to be said now. I want to go to sleep,' he interrupted her a little later. As far as he was concerned that was the end of it and he was feeling far too relaxed and contented to pay much attention to Natasha's determined efforts to bring a few of her psychological insights to bear on the situation. 'Look, I really think we can sort all this out sometime tomorrow – you seem to forget that I have to go to the library in the morning and I shall never be able to work if my head isn't fresh.' Why, he was practically rebuking her! He turned his face to the wall and wrapped himself up more tightly in the blanket, while Natasha lay on her back, her hands clasped behind her head, thinking. At last she was beginning to understand the bitterness which so often took hold of her at these times, although this didn't make it any easier to bear the devastatingly abrupt way his attitude to her changed after they made love. Afterwards, he was like a different person, remote and unloving, whereas with her it was completely the other way round. Passionate and joyful lovemaking always swept her away on a tide of tender emotions to the point where she felt they had become one person.

Now she gazed despondently at the back of his head. How sweet that dear familiar head of his was to her, for all that she felt so crushed and downcast. She kissed it gently and then, very carefully, got out of the bed. 'Sleep well, Senechka, I think we'd sleep better in our own beds. Will you kiss me before I go?' she whispered, leaning over him.

'What's up, Natasha?' he murmured, half-asleep. 'Surely that's enough kisses for one night – why, you're insatiable, woman! Or are you ill?'

Natasha recoiled in horror. His words struck her like blows across the face. How could he so horribly misinterpret her feelings, so completely fail to understand her unsatisfied desire for some warmth and tenderness! So, left with nothing but a cold and lonely longing, she was to leave his room feeling more cheated, more numb, than when she had gone in!

Slowly, deep in thought, Natasha put her dressing-gown on again and set off once more down the endless corridor with its awful red carpet. At the corner there was a little table at which the night-porter sat dozing. As she passed him, he woke and eyed her brazenly, muttering something under his breath. She didn't hear what he said but it was undoubtedly some obscenity. She hunched her shoulders and made her way back to her room.

* X *

Natasha's stay in G'ville was rapidly turning into a kind of voluntary incarceration. In the early days of their love affair she'd found it quite exciting to wait like a captive for Senya to arrive, in some secret hiding-place. She'd called him her 'pasha', and had referred to herself as the 'odalisk of the harem', the special attraction of this game being the complete break that it made with the frantic bustle of her life at home. When she met Senya she became invisible to the world of politics and people, and she loved surrendering her name and identity when she went incognito to meet him. Nor did she have to worry too much about her friends in the Party, who were generally most understanding about her tendency to disappear rather frequently at short notice. Some thought that she was fulfilling family obligations, and others simply assumed she'd been summoned to carry out Party work in another town. Up till now, the break with everyday life had always been a welcome rest.

But this time in G'ville she found her role as 'odalisk of the harem' both irksome and irritating. She couldn't walk down the street for fear of meeting someone she knew. She couldn't even sit for an hour or so in the hotel dining-room in case Senya dashed back and, not finding her in her room, went straight off again. For Natasha the time hung heavy, empty and dull. Days dragged aimlessly by and she had little to do but wait.

Senya, on the other hand, was anxious not to waste one minute of his time in G'ville. He was totally absorbed in his work, but even more obsessively absorbed – or so it seemed to Natasha – in the professor, with whose large and hospitable family he began to spend more and more of his time. Even when they were drinking their coffee together in the morning he'd constantly be glancing at his watch, anxious that he might be late. He invariably dined at the professor's house and whiled away most of his evenings there too, so that soon he could only spare the odd moment here and there for Natasha, when he'd dash over to see her under the pretext of important letters to be written or material to be collected. He was always exceptionally lively during these brief snatched encounters with her, lounging on the sofa as he chatted away about this and that, recounting various trivial anecdotes about the professor and his work.

On one occasion he deigned to let her make him some tea and she improvised a feast for both of them, with Gervaise cheese, fruit and jam. She listened to him carefully as she bustled about preparing it, not wanting to miss a word he was saying. Naturally it delighted her that he seemed so happy and everything was going so well for him. Nevertheless an evil worm was at work within her. It was so rarely now that he told her about his work. And he was less forthcoming these days with stories about the professor too, though Natasha was past caring about that. Her antipathy towards 'that old archive rat', ran deeper and deeper, and she continued to find it quite incomprehensible that Senya should consider him brilliant merely because he was so learned. How could Senya be so naive?

'I just don't understand you, Senya!' she burst out as she was pouring the tea. 'You open your mind to the professor in this completely infantile fashion, you reveal to him all the ideas you've been working on and haven't fully thought through, and next thing you know he'll be making use of them, amplifying them with all that academic erudition of his, presenting them as his own. Meanwhile you'll still be sweating it out and trying to finish your book.' She spoke calmly to make doubly sure that her words went home and hurt him, as she intended them to.

'Really Natasha, what silly things you do say. Quite frankly, you sometimes remind me of Anyuta. Now have you ever heard of colleagues and friends in the same line of academic work stealing ideas from each other?'

'I certainly have! Surely you're not trying to tell me such things don't happen – why, I can think of countless cases! And if you think they don't, you're just being foolish and naive.'

Senya continued to protest, but Natasha knew that she'd succeeded in kindling a spark of suspicion in his mind, and this gave her some small sense of malicious satisfaction. But after he'd left she suddenly felt what a very mean thing she'd done to him, and felt quite appalled at herself. She could only wonder at what was at the root of her desire to denigrate the professor in his eyes. What else but jealousy! She finally began to understand something of what Anyuta must have been feeling, and what made her act so hysterically. She felt disgusted with herself, longing to make amends, but realised all too sickeningly clearly that what had been said couldn't be unsaid. 'God, how vile of me, there's no end to the damage I might have done ... ' And from that day she responded particularly appreciatively to Senya's endless lyrical praise of the professor and his family, hoping that if *she* talked enthusiastically enough about all the professor's sterling qualities she might drive out the worm of distrust she'd implanted in Senya's mind.

But her resentment was still very much alive. Every morning she'd get up with high hopes of Senya devoting the whole day to her – well not the whole day perhaps, maybe just a few peaceful hours in which they'd be together and talk about their feelings. But as one day followed another it soon became clear that this time would just not be found. In the brief moments when they did meet during the day they'd hug and kiss, there'd be much laughing and joking over tea, and at night they'd fall into each other's arms and embrace passionately, but somehow they never did manage to find time to talk. Natasha tried to do some work on a pamphlet for which she had a deadline, but found the whole project so daunting that she made hardly any progress with it. She might put a few thoughts together in the course of one day, but when she looked her writing over the next day it never seemed satisfactory, and her style seemed laboured, completely lacking in verve. She was surprised and hurt, too, that Senya did not once ask her how her work was going.

They were killing time. Precious time was trickling through their fingers, wasted on trivial, futile things . . .

* XI *

One day a large bundle of business and personal letters arrived at the hotel for Natasha, forwarded to her by a roundabout route. The letters, related to Party business, contained some shocking news about two of her comrades who had 'fallen ill' (in Party code this meant that they'd been arrested). Their 'illness', it was feared, might well be prolonged, and would certainly have serious consequences for everyone associated with them. Natasha was deeply upset, and especially upset to be kicking her heels in G'ville in this crisis. What was she doing here anyway? Was it for *his* sake or hers that she was staying on? She neither knew nor cared. She knew that she could never leave him with so much coldness in her heart, and that it would do her no good to go before expressing at least some of her resentment. She'd only suffer afterwards. No, she really must speak to him.

Today she'd try to find the words to describe something of what she felt. The problem was that she didn't really know *what* there was to describe. But she was determined to break down the barrier between them so she could leave calm in the knowledge that there was still some friendship and understanding between them. She waited with mounting impatience for him to return.

That day of all days, Senya was extremely late back. When he did eventually return, some time after midnight, it was straight from a large dinner-party given specially in his honour at the professor's house, and he was very drunk and merry. 'Well, they fed and watered us until we burst,' he announced, oblivious to Natasha's glowering look, 'and I'm afraid I've had one too many. Never mind, it'll pass. So what about you, my love? Been bored?' He nuzzled her cheek, kissed her ear.

'Please Senya, not just now.' She extricated herself from his arms. 'I want to tell you about some letters I got this morning: Katerina Petrovna and Nikanor have both been arrested.'

'I don't believe it, oh God, how frightful!'

'I'm so terribly sad for both of them – what a ghastly mess, what a tragedy ... ' And before she could stop herself she had collapsed in tears. She was actually sobbing more for herself than for her friends, but these distinctions were becoming increasingly blurred, for her emotions were in chaos, life was a dismal burden and the future seemed to hold out nothing but a long chain of humiliations and misfortunes. What had been the purpose of that brave new course on which she and the others had launched the Party? What had possessed her to leave them, when her place was so obviously with them?

'Come, Natasha dear, do stop crying. You really can't let something like this get you down so much.' He spoke wearily, reproachfully, as if he had already had more than he could endure of women's tears. 'You never know, there may still be something we can do.'

'Like what, for instance? But anyway, it's not that I'm crying for, it's everything about this wasted life of ours which is nothing but misery and pain.'

'Yes, but then you know as well as I do that you always run that kind of risk when you do political work. Now when I was working underground in the Volga region . . . ' Senya assumed that Natasha was lamenting the hardship of Party work and felt that the best way to distract her was by recounting some of the dangers from his own revolutionary past. But Natasha had already heard all these stories of arrest, exile and escape, and listened with only half an ear. Her mind was too full of the misgivings and anxieties she was determined to talk about.

' . . . So all I'm saying is that we've always run these sorts of risks and had to cope with these crises,' he concluded, 'and yet look at me – I'm still alive, aren't I? And I haven't even lost the ability to fall deeply in love with a very beautiful woman, eh Natasha? Are you listening to me, Natasha?'

'Yes, yes, I'm listening Senya, it's just that I've had other things on my mind. There's something I want to tell you. I've decided to go back tomorrow. I can't sit around here and do nothing any longer . . . '

'But that's the most ridiculous thing I've ever heard! This is the very time you *shouldn't* go back. You're sure to put your foot in it and end up in trouble yourself, and I shall do my damndest to see you don't return. Please Natasha, be sensible, let the dust settle a bit before you go. They don't need you, not at the moment anyway. They'll manage perfectly well without you.'

Natasha hotly contradicted him and they began to argue fiercely. It was more important to her than almost anything else that Senya should recognise the value of her political work, and especially important now that she was about to leave him. But he would only keep stubbornly repeating how childish and ridiculous she was being. 'As if they can't find other people to do your work while you're here! Believe me, anyone could do that work – as well or better than you!'

He wouldn't listen to her. She actually quoted, word for word, her friends' urgent requests for her to return, but these he dismissed. 'Yes, and who is that writing? Maria Mikhailovna? I might have known! Why she's nothing but a hysterical woman who's always moaning about something. Now I'd understand how you were feeling if it was Dontsov writing, because he knows his stuff. That really would mean something – but Maria Mikhailovna, who gives a toss what *she* thinks? I wouldn't get into a state about anything *she* says if I were you.'

She felt quite unable to defend herself against these hurtful words. She had to admit that she *was* disappointed that it wasn't Dontsov (the man with the limp) who was urging her to return. That would have proved beyond any doubt that her friends genuinely did need and value her work, and then, oh then Natasha would have flown straight back to them, without another thought. All right, she was offended that Dontsov hadn't been amongst those begging her to return, she admitted that. But why couldn't Senya be a little more sympathetic and why did he always have to rub these things in? Why did he invariably fail to listen to her or understand what was going on in her mind? Did he actually intend to hurt her . . . ?

She said goodnight to him coldly, hoping that he might notice and respond in some way. But he was apparently quite oblivious to her icy manner. He retired to his room and left Natasha alone, assailed by a deep and all-too-familiar fear of her solitude – a fear, mainly, of her own unstated and unacknowledged grievances. Come what may, they'd have to break this awful silence and have it out. Either he'd understand what she was talking about or it would be the end of their relationship. Anything would be better than this silence which starved the spirit. She opened her door and hurried towards his room. 'Thank god I only have to be here until tomorrow − I couldn't endure another long pointless day in this place,' she thought.

As she reached his door she paused and put her ear to the keyhole. She could hear nothing. Senya must be sleeping. He always fell asleep the moment his head touched the pillow. She turned the door handle a little, then released it. Suddenly she could imagine the sleepy expression on his face as she opened the door, and she flushed with shame as she imagined what he'd say to her. 'Aha, so you've come again! What am I going to do with you? I'm tired, can't you get that into your head? Whatever will I do tomorrow if my head isn't fresh . . . ?'

'No, please no,' she whispered, 'I couldn't bear all that again.' She ran back down the corridor to her room. The night porter was puzzled and fascinated. The lady had obviously changed her mind. 'Must've quarrelled, I suppose,' he muttered, grinning, as she passed him.

* XII *

Senya left the hotel first thing in the morning and didn't look in once to see her during the entire day, something he'd never done before. By evening she was getting worried. She lost count of the number of times she opened the door of her room to listen and peer out into the empty, dimly lit corridor. Once the silence was broken by the sound of someone clearing his throat; a man's footsteps turned into the corridor and her heart leapt. But it wasn't him.

By three in the morning she was almost demented with anxiety, convinced that he must have had an accident. He'd never stayed out so late before. She kept hoping that he had in fact got back and gone straight to bed without coming in to see her. Again and again she set off down the corridor to his room and, finding it empty, retraced her steps. The night-porter, more fascinated than ever, eyed her and smirked offensively. But such irritations were as nothing compared to her anxieties about Senya.

He could at least have telephoned to tell her what was happening. He might have lost track of the time while he was talking to the professor and decided to spend the night there, but she could hardly believe that he'd completely forget about her – that would be unforgivable of him. He must know how worried she'd be. He would never do such a thing to Anyuta. The hours passed, her fantasies of what might have happened grew, and soon she was nearly beside herself with anxiety. She tried to rest, yet no sooner had she stretched herself out on her bed than she'd be leaping up to open the door. But still the same dreary silence. There was never a soul to be seen in that ill-lit corridor with the loathsome red carpet – if it hadn't been for that awful carpet she'd be able to hear his footsteps from far away.

Someone coughed a few doors away, someone snored sweetly – then there was silence again, broken only by the clock on the tower opposite striking four-thirty. Her vigil was becoming unbearable. She longed for morning. Her only hope now was that he'd decided to spend the night at the professor's. She could just picture him running back to her shamefaced in the morning, making a lot of silly excuses like a naughty child. 'But how could I have telephoned?' he'd say. 'The professor would have guessed everything.' He'd stand there, looking ashamed of himself and waiting for her to tell him off, but she'd only smile at him in her usual mild manner, and stroke back his untidy forelock to kiss his brow.

'You don't have to explain anything to me, Senya, I do understand,' she'd say, and he'd sigh with relief; 'You're so good to me, Natasha ... ' Then they'd both feel instantly cheerful again, and all her fears would seem foolish ...
'I'm just on edge.' She tried now to reassure herself. 'There's no earthly reason to assume anything terrible has happened. And I can get some sleep while I'm waiting. I won't lock the door.' So she forced herself to lie down for a while and even managed to doze for a while. But even as she dozed she was perpetually listening for his footsteps. There was the faintest hint of a rustle outside: in an instant she had leapt out of bed, her heart thumping wildly. But no, it was only the couple in the room next door brushing against the adjoining wall. She heard some people exchanging a few words with the hall porter, and once again she was wide awake ...

Soon it was nine o'clock, and a dull grey morning light crept through the blinds into her room. Unable to stay in bed a moment longer, she got up and dressed with deliberate slowness, still intensely alert to every sound. She opened the door into the corridor just one more time, but now that the lights had been switched off it looked even more desolate. Again and again she peered out, even though part of her knew she was being ridiculous. She just kept on hoping that at any minute that dear familiar figure in the battered soft cap would appear round the bend in the corridor. This night had proved to her just how precious and necessary her Senya was to her!

She reproached herself for all her grievances, and she bitterly regretted all the unkind thoughts she'd ever had about him, all the times in the past when she'd hurt his feelings. Now she longed only for him to come back so that she could know he was safe and well.

Of course – he might have returned after she'd gone to bed! The moment this happy thought flashed into her mind she ran down the corridor, her hair streaming down her back, comb in hand. Several people had to step quickly out of her way as she rushed past, and she brushed against the woman washing the floor, splashing water on to the carpet as she did so. She stopped to apologise profusely. The woman grumbled and moved her bucket.

Senya's room was empty, his bed unslept in. Non-plussed, Natasha sank down on to it to wait for him, for she felt closer to him sitting there surrounded by his things – that familiar old pair of trousers and that waistcoat . . .

She realised now what must have happened. Anyuta had arrived in G'ville unexpectedly, and Senya must be out of his mind with worry lest the two of them should accidentally meet. If this was so, Natasha really ought to leave town. But then she did so want to be of some comfort to Senya – or at least to let him know she was leaving, so that he wouldn't have to worry about bringing Anyuta to the hotel. It occurred to her that she might phone the professor, then realised Anyuta might well be there. Anyway, she'd been strictly forbidden to use the telephone. But what if Senya was at this very moment on his way to the hotel with Anyuta? Galvanised by the thought, she leapt off the bed, swiftly scrutinised the room for any evidence of her presence, and then poked her head out of the door to make sure the corridor was empty before hurrying back to her room.

The clock struck ten. The clock struck eleven, and twelve, and one . . . By now Natasha had long ceased to wait or listen, and had abandoned all hope of ever seeing him again. He might have been arrested. He might have had an accident (he was so short-sighted it was quite possible that he'd been run over and seriously hurt). He might be dead. Of course, he just *might* be alive and well somewhere – but if he was, surely he'd have found some way of getting a brief message to her and putting her mind at rest? This endless silence must mean that something deeply and irreparably terrible had happened to him.

Natasha slumped in a chair with her eyes closed, for the daylight irritated them unbearably. In the long hours of the night she had longed for the day, but now she longed for darkness to come again. In the dark it had at least been possible to hope. Now all hope was gone. Maybe he was in hospital and nobody knew where he was, maybe he was calling for her. If he hadn't come back by three that afternoon (this was the time he generally called back at the hotel to see her), she would phone the professor – and damn the consequences. She felt much better after making this decision, and began to move about the room tidying things away. Then, just when she'd finally persuaded herself to stop waiting for him, there was a loud rap at the door.

'Come in!' she called out, freezing with sudden apprehension. A young messenger-boy handed her a letter. She seized it from him, struggled with the envelope and tore out a letter from Senya.

'I'm afraid something most unpleasant and unexpected has happened to me. Last night, shortly after dinner, I began to have the most excruciating stomach-ache, and I was soon feeling so ill that I had to go to bed. My temperature shot up and they called the doctor, who feared it might be appendicitis. By then the pain was indescribable and I had to have two morphine injections.

'Today, thank heavens, I'm feeling a lot better. The doctor's just been, and he says I'll pull through and there won't be any need to operate. My temperature's lower but still above normal. I'm still in a great deal of pain, but at least it is bearable now. I just need complete peace and quiet and a good rest.

'I do hope you won't worry too much about me. I must say this could hardly have happened in a better place, here with the professor and his family. D'you know, they stayed up all night looking after me?

'I've told them that I met this Russian family, old friends of mine, in the hotel, and that I wanted to ask them to choose a few books to send me. That was the excuse I gave them for writing to you. So do you think you could just send me whatever comes easiest to hand? I don't actually feel up to reading just now, so it really doesn't matter what. But one thing I do beg of you: please don't under any circumstances phone or write to me here. I kiss your hands.

Senya.'

Poor, poor Senechka....

The little messenger-boy, who had been quietly waiting while she read this letter through, was becoming impatient. 'Will there be any reply then?' he asked.

'A reply? Oh yes, of course. Would you mind sitting down for a moment while I sort out some books for you to take back?'

She hurried off to his room, too numb to grasp anything properly but the fact that she must find some books for him but not write to him. Yet how she yearned to write to him, even one line, just to let him know how much she had worried about him, how much she loved him. She did hope he wasn't too anxious about her. Everything seemed bearable now she knew he was alive. But despite her relief she was trembling so much that she could hardly get her fingers to make the books into a parcel. Just a little note in the parcel! She was almost demented with frustration at being denied this one small pleasure. She knew as well as he did that she couldn't, though – they'd only see it and ask him all sorts of embarrassing questions, and poor dear Senya, who was such a bad liar, would be sure to betray his confusion. She certainly had no wish to put him through all

104

that. She handed the books over to the messenger-boy who went off at once, leaving her alone once more in her tiny single room.

Her morning coffee, still undrunk, stood on the little table by the sofa. The melancholy which had settled within her was every bit as sour and cold as those muddy dregs, a depression compounded of her worst fears and regrets.

The danger wasn't over yet. The doctor's words were of small consolation to her when she thought of Senya, writhing in agony. How could she complain of her own foolish miseries in the face of pain, fever, morphine? No, this was real suffering, making her own seem pale and petty by comparison, and obliterating all her worries of the past few days.

* XIII *

Two long, empty days passed; three nights filled with hours of anxious solitary reflection and exhaustingly vivid dreams from which she was invariably jolted awake with the same question on her lips: 'Senya! Where are you? What are you doing?' Once she dreamed very clearly that she heard Senya's voice, and woke up terrified that this might be some kind of omen. She ran downstairs several times each day to the hotel porter in the hope of finding a letter or a telephone message for her, or perhaps just a little note delivered by the messenger-boy. Behind her back the hotel servants whispered and sniggered amongst themselves: to her face they respectfully enquired whether the monsieur was reserving the room or whether he'd left for good.

Naturally he'd reserved it, she told them; it was simply

that monsieur was ill, and it was more convenient that he should recover with friends. She found it extremely irritating to have to go into all this – why should she be made to feel she had to justify herself in this way when all she cared about was how Senya was? There was no longer any doubt in her mind that he'd taken a turn for the worse. He must be very sick indeed not to have found *some* way of getting in touch with her. She longed only to know that he was alive.

Long listless hours dragged by and on the third day she was beginning to feel utterly desperate. She'd imagine that several hours had gone by, only to realise that the clock hand had moved just one minute. She was incapable of doing any work, and unable to leave the building in case there was a message for her. Towards the evening of that day she felt she hadn't the strength to endure any more. The prospect of another long night on her own terrified her. She no longer cared about the consequences – she'd get the porter to phone the professor and find out how he was.

Trembling with fear, she rang the bell for room-service. What if her message got garbled? What if Anyuta was there? An endless series of dreadful possibilities flashed through her mind ...

'*Que desire madame?*' The porter arrived promptly in response to her call, but she felt this was merely calculated to startle and confuse her. At that moment her mind was a complete blank and she had no idea what to do next. So she merely asked him for some tea. The porter enquired whether she wanted lemon or milk, flashed his little white napkin, and was off. She paced listlessly around the room, groaning and wringing her hands, her aching head filled with ghastly images. The tea arrived, the clock struck nine, and her last hope for some message from Senya faded. She rang a second time, more decisively now. But this time the porter took his time in coming, and when he did arrive he stood looking bored and shuffling his feet. Little did he know what a

106

struggle it was to appear calm! She asked him if he would kindly make a phone call for her. She told him as clearly as she could the questions she wanted him to ask. 'You don't have to mention it's a woman asking, though,' she added hastily, 'just say it's his Russian friends who are worried about him and would like some news.'

'I understand perfectly, madame,' the porter said suavely, and hurried off bearing a scrap of paper with his instructions.

'I just hope to God he doesn't get it wrong and reveal that it's a woman asking him to make the call ... ' This was all that seemed important to her as she waited in a fever of agitation for him to return. She prayed that everything would go smoothly, that nothing would happen to distress Senya. She stopped pacing about the room and sat down on the edge of the sofa. Her heart seemed to be beating in her throat; she had difficulty in swallowing; she was as tense as a violin string. Any second now she'd know the worst.

Five minutes, seven minutes, ten minutes dragged by – how unbearably long he was taking, why hadn't he come back yet? He must have some message so terrible that he couldn't bring himself to tell her. The very idea made her practically faint from fear. An icy shiver gripped her. She knew suddenly that in an hour, by which time she'd know all, she would look back with longing at this tortured respite. At least some hope was still alive and warm within her ...

There was a knock at the door. 'Come in!' She managed to call out only with the greatest difficulty. The porter stood in the doorway and she fixed desperate beseeching eyes on him. But he was in no hurry to deliver his message – the way his napkin was arranged on his arm was not precisely to his liking, and his first concern at that moment was to put it straight. At last, he spoke: 'I am told to inform you that the monsieur thanks his Russian friends' (he smirked beneath his little moustache) 'for their concern. He is feeling very much better today. He has taken a walk around his room and is now about to retire to sleep.'

Natasha sat motionless and silent.

'That is the end of the message. Will there be anything else, madame?'

'No thank you, nothing else.'

Whisking his white napkin he went off. How funny, she'd thought that if the porter had brought back hopeful news, some ray of light, however feeble, she'd burst into tears of joy. A year ago she would have endured anything just to know he was well. Now she stood stock-still in the middle of the room in a state of shock. She no longer understood anything. Certainly she no longer understood Senya. Tormented and distraught, she was cut to the quick by feelings of bitterness that were quite new to her. Senya, who was afraid of inflicting the slightest pain on Anyuta, had made not the slightest move to put an end to her torment. Dear gentle Senya indeed! How dare he behave like this, and how dare he pretend that he still loved her? She tossed back her head in that characteristically proud gesture of hers, as though Senya were in the room to see her. She would never, never forget the insulting way he had just treated her.

* XIV *

Natasha slept soundly that night and awoke refreshed, untroubled and determined to ignore the last lingering traces of last night's misery. There was little point in being sad anyway, now that the danger was over and Senya was alive and on the way to recovery. Any day now she'd be seeing him again, and then she'd tell him very plainly what a terrible thing it was to treat love so carelessly. She'd explain to him that if you stretched a person's heart-strings too far, love would die.

This was the first morning since her arrival when Natasha actually enjoyed her coffee. She smiled warmly at the chambermaid who brought it and stayed to tell her what a wonderful spring day it was and how madame must be sure to go out for a walk. If only she was free like madame, sighed the girl, she'd be outside, walking from morning to night.

Natasha read through her business letters, and for the first time in many days felt able to attend to them with the seriousness they demanded. She felt ashamed to have fallen so badly behind with her correspondence. In no time at all she had a large bundle of letters written, and no sooner had she cleared these out of the way than the urge came upon her to do some work on her pamphlet which had lain virtually untouched in her drawer. Now, for the first time in G'ville, she was able to write with her customary fluency. The right words, clear and precise, presented themselves at once to her mind and poured from her pen arranging themselves into a neat logical chain of ideas. Before she knew it the whole day had passed and it was getting dark. She had finished the first chapter.

She stretched blissfully, and felt remarkably happy and clear-headed. She had made a start on the pamphlet, and she didn't have to worry about Senya any more or wait for the phone to ring. He was probably having the time of his life at the professor's house! He'd obviously have no time to spare a thought for Natasha. Sad, really. But she quickly shook the thought off, for after the stress of the last few days the muscles of her soul needed some relaxation. What she wanted now was to escape for a while from this ridiculous imprisoned existence, and make for some cheerful place where she'd be surrounded by people and movement and light. She decided to drop off some letters at the post-office and go on from there to some brightly lit café where she could sit and drink a cup of hot chocolate. She'd just put on her hat and veil when the door opened and, without so much as a knock, Semyon Semyonovich burst in.

'Senya!' she gasped, more in amazement than joy, 'what are *you* doing here?'

'Oh I'm exhausted, Natasha, this illness really has taken it out of me. But I had to drag myself over here to see you, even though the doctor did urge me to wait till tomorrow. You see I just couldn't wait that long ... '

'But you must lie down at once Senya – oh how thin you've got and how ill you look, your eyes are so hollow ... Whatever made you come here, darling?'

'I was getting so restless, Natasha, I had so much on my mind ... '

'Now just let me get you a pillow and I'll take your boots off for you. You lie down here and I'll put this blanket over you. Would you like some tea perhaps? With lemon or milk? I'll just ring and order it for you ... ' Natasha hoped that if she busied herself like this she might conceal the sad fact that there was none of that dizzy joy she'd expected to feel when she saw him. She'd pictured this moment so many times, imagined herself rushing into his arms to hug him and kiss his hands. ... Now she hadn't the slightest desire to do so, Senya had come back at quite the most inopportune moment, and had completely destroyed the calm abandon she'd been feeling.

'Please don't put yourself out on my account, Natashechka dear. Why don't you sit down here beside me instead of rushing about? Oh, I've missed you so much ... But whatever are you doing with your hat on? About to sneak out, were you? And might I ask where? So you've been gadding about while I've been away ill, have you? Well madam, I earnestly hope you've managed to preserve your incognito in the process.' The rebuke beneath this clumsy joke was badly concealed.

'No no, this is the first time, Senya. I swear I haven't so much as poked my nose out of doors all this time. But now I really ought to because these letters here have piled up so. I was just off to the post-office to mail them by special delivery.'

'But isn't that really rather rash, especially now, when Anyuta might arrive at any moment? And why, Natasha, did you have to phone the professor's house when I specifically asked you not to? I never realised my wishes meant so little to you. All the time I've been ill I haven't had a moment's peace, worrying that you'd phone, and when you did I knew I'd have to drag myself out of bed and get over here, even if it killed me. Why, for all I knew, you might have decided to visit the professor's house ... '

'Wait a moment,' Natasha's voice trembled with rage. 'Tell me, is that the only reason you've come to see me today? Because you were afraid I might visit the professor's house?'

'No, of course that's not the only reason,' he said, sensing now how deeply angry she was. 'I missed you, Natashenka, surely I don't have to tell you that.'

'Hah, so you missed me! What a joke!' He'd never heard her laugh like that before and he found it profoundly disturbing. 'You missed me after you'd devised the cruellest possible way of torturing me ... '

'Stop that, Natasha, what on earth is wrong with you? Why, that could have been Anyuta speaking just now. Do you realise what you're saying? Surely you're not blaming me for being ill? *How* did I torture you, Natasha, tell me, what have I done? I don't understand, I didn't mean to hurt you ... Oh Natasha, I do love you so much – but then maybe Anyuta's right and I only hurt the people I love most, Anyuta, you ... Oh god, how hard it all is ... '

111

Senya buried his face in his hands and looked so genuinely grief-stricken and vulnerable that Natasha's heart went out to him at once. 'Oh Senechka, forgive me, I don't know what possessed me to say that. I've been at the end of my tether these past few days, terrified you might die, with nothing to do here but brood and imagine the worst. And I do love you, do you hear me, Simeon?' This was her special name for him. He looked up at once with that bright untroubled smile of his and Natasha, kneeling on the floor before him, kissed his head. 'Now let me kiss your hands, Senya, oh how I've dreamed of seeing you again – and d'you know, I dreamt the first thing I'd do would be to kiss your hands.'

'You're a sweet thing, Natasha – but how you did frighten me with that weird laugh of yours just now. Poor dear, I know your nerves are on edge, like mine. What a hard life it is ... But what are you doing, squeezing me so tight?'

'I feel so happy now that you're here, *all* of you – you know what I mean, don't you?'

'Indeed I do darling, but I'm afraid I'm still very weak and I just get over-excited when you hold me so tight. You know, the doctor said my illness was probably nervous in origin, and that all I need now is plenty of rest. Please don't be offended if I ask you to move away a little.'

Natasha got up and moved away, turning her face so he shouldn't see the hurt in her eyes. All she'd longed for was some physical warmth from him, some human contact. How could he have misinterpreted her desires so dreadfully? She poured tea for him and he lit a cigarette, lay back on the sofa and launched into a long discourse on the professor's family and how very affectionately they'd looked after him. He told her too how very anxious he'd been, afraid that she'd come to the house, and how frustrated he'd been at being unable to communicate with her.

At this she raised her eyebrows. 'But you might have sent

me a little note, some little message after I'd sent you those books. Surely you could have thought something up ... '

'But you know what a hopelessly bad liar I am, and then I *did* drag myself here to see you as soon as I was strong enough.'

As they drank their tea Natasha told him about the letters she'd received, and about the latest developments within the Party. Much of the news was depressing, for the political heat was really on now. But there was much that was encouraging too, various exciting new developments. Senya and Natasha were soon deep in political discussion, going over all the possible tactics suggested by their friends, drawing up resolutions, outlining their next campaign, and trying to anticipate the opposition's next move – the situation would precipitate new conflicts. Suddenly Party work seemed exciting again, and they both found themselves longing to get back to it.

'Oh lord!' Senya broke off. 'It's all play and no work here. With you time does fly so, and I forget everything that's going on in the outside world. I promised I'd be home, the professor's home I mean, by half-past seven and look, it's already eight. I do hope they're not worrying about me, because they might just run over here to find out what's happening.'

'You're leaving? You're spending the night there?'

'Yes, I'm afraid they just won't hear of me staying the night at the hotel. I must collect my things and dash back now. But Natashechka, I do want to say one thing to you before I go.' She knew something unpleasant was to follow from the way he avoided her eyes. 'I want to put it to you that you might like to visit the town of B'ere.'

'But why should I want to visit that place?'

'Well, it's apparently a fascinating old town, full of ancient buildings, and you know how much you love that sort of thing,' he said, pleading with her as one might coax a child to take its medicine.

'I don't understand what you're talking about.'

'Oh never mind, I can see you don't want to go.' He glanced guiltily at her. 'Look, the fact of the matter is that at the moment, with you here, I can't relax for a moment. I had to write to Anyuta when I was ill, and, well, you know Anyuta. For all I know she may turn up here at any moment. That's why I think it would be much less anxious and fraught for us all.'

Natasha bowed her head and two large tears dropped into her still undrunk tea. 'Ah, my poor sweet girl,' Senya stroked her hair. 'I do know how hard it is for you to leave me.' He spoke tenderly, but at that moment his compassion merely seemed patronising to her.

'But why should I leave for B'ere anyway? I might as well go straight home instead.' Natasha's tears had dried. She looked at him calmly and somewhat distantly.

'But you don't understand, I wasn't asking you to leave for good, just for a little while, just for the next few days. You see, there's a holiday here at the end of the week and the library will be closed, and I've already dropped a few hints about the possibility of my visiting B'ere, told the professor I wanted to see the town and so on. If you go now, I'll follow on in a few days and meet you there.'

'No, that's too ridiculous for words. If I'm in your way here I should go straight back home.'

'But how could you think such a thing! You're not in my way! It's only because of Anyuta that I'm suggesting this, you know. Imagine her coming here and making trouble – that's why I'm so anxious at the moment.' He grew more confident, convinced by his own arguments. 'Anyway we shan't be seeing very much of each other as it is, because I agreed to leave the hotel for the professor's house today. If you do go to B'ere we'll only have to wait till Friday. Then we'll be able to spend some time together and relax, without work or the professor to distract us. Doesn't that appeal to you?'

'But you're forgetting something. I have to be back by next Tuesday at the very latest.'

'Well why don't we see how it goes between now and then? If everything still seems fairly quiet at your end surely you can snatch a day or two more. I do think it's important for us to have a few uninterrupted, restful days together – I'll feel quite different when I know that neither the professor nor anyone else is around. At the moment I'm constantly on edge – why, at this very moment they might be on their way to look for me.'

'All right then, I'll think about it and we can talk about it tomorrow,' conceded Natasha grudgingly.

'No no, tomorrow's no good, you must leave today, without fail! I've already checked the trains and written them down somewhere ... now wait a moment, let me find them for you,' he scanned his notebook shortsightedly. 'Yes, here we are. If you get the 10.30 train tonight you'll be there in just an hour and a half. Isn't that convenient? That's the fast train, you'll catch it without any problem. Now don't look so miserable, Natashenka, or I'll believe I've done something terrible to hurt you. I'm sad too, you know, that we have to part like this, but I just remind myself that it won't be very long till we see each other again. When you get there, book a double room, tell them you're waiting for your husband and send me a telegram signed with the usual initials, care of the post office here, to tell me which hotel you're at.' He clearly felt all this would be some sort of consolation for her. 'Now be a dear and help me with my packing will you? I must be off. And oh yes, will you settle up with the hotel? You know how bad I am at that sort of thing. D'you need some cash? Because if you do, the professor's offered me some ... Please don't look so wretched, Natasha, I just can't bear it.'

'Don't you worry about me, Senya, I'll get over it. Now lie down here while I go and pack your things. No, I'll do it, you mustn't tire yourself, you're not well. That's it, you just lie down.' Natasha ran off.

She was just strapping up his hold-all when he crept in stealthily, making her start. 'Whatever are you doing here, Senechka? You should be lying down. Look, I've finished your packing.'

'I was so worried,' he cast a guilty troubled look at her. 'I was afraid you might be sitting in here on your own and crying. I do love you, Natasha, very, very much.' He said this so solemnly that she couldn't help smiling. But her feelings were numb, her mind a complete blank. She didn't know whether he really loved her or not, or what love meant to him anyway. And what did it mean for her, apart from pain, humiliation, worry ...

'Come on and get dressed, Senechka, otherwise you'll be late for dinner at the professor's and you wouldn't want Mrs Professor to tell you off, would you?'

'Ah, come now, you wouldn't be jealous of her, would you? She's an old lady!'

Natasha smiled again. 'You know Senechka you're really so childish sometimes, you funny man. It's amazing, the things you don't understand! Anyway, the main thing is for you to look after yourself and make sure you don't fall ill again. I've put your manuscript in its file and the books are here. Goodbye now, Senechka.' They embraced.

'You kissed me so coldly then,' he looked sadly at her, 'as if your heart wasn't in it.'

'I'm just behaving like a virtuous little wife; I wouldn't want to seduce you, after all,' Natasha laughed, as she hurried off to call a porter to carry Senya's bags downstairs.

'We must order a car to take you there so you don't wear yourself out.'

In the corridor Senya embraced her impulsively and whispered in her ear: 'Please don't be angry with me, my dear, you're the woman I love. You can't imagine how much I need you. Believe me, all this is only because I'm afraid Anyuta may come.'

When they reached the turn in the corridor he stopped and gazed silently at her, shaking his head as though he longed to tell her something and explain himself to her. But she merely laughed and flapped the ends of her scarf in his face: 'Now don't you go falling in love with the professor's wife, and come and see me soon!' At this he grinned at her, visibly relaxed. The next moment he was striding purposefully off down the corridor. Natasha bowed her head pensively and retraced her steps along that all too horribly familiar carpet to her room.

* XV *

B'ere was indeed a beautiful old town. Its quiet, ancient streets and ornately decorated churches attracted quite a number of tourists, so that when Natasha arrived she had no difficulty in finding herself a comfortable room in a cheap hotel. She loved the room immediately. It was furnished simply in a modern uncluttered style, without the usual dust-traps like heavy carpets and velvet curtains, and had a pleasantly soothing effect on her.

More important, as she discovered the moment she woke up next morning, it was flooded with sunlight. The view from the window, unlike the dark roofs and small courtyard in G'ville, was on to a broad, quiet square lined with old houses in which countless generations had lived and died. She got up, raised the blind and smiled at the warm spring sun with a sense of joy. She felt cheerful and energetic. Everything pleased her: the comfortable bed, the capacious wash-stand and, most of all, the view. She flung open the window and a soft breeze, fragrant with sweet spring flowers, caressed her face. A chorus of birds rose from the garden below.

'How wonderful life is! And to think how anxious I was! What was it all for ... ?'

She started eagerly on her work, and from the moment she sat down it went easily and quickly, without any sense of strain. She wrote all day and when evening came she was sorry to tear herself away, for she felt she could have written all night too. But she did want to see the lovely old town, and wandered out to gaze at B'ere's dreaming buildings, towers, domes and lacey cathedrals. She delighted in her new-found freedom like a schoolgirl on holiday. She was very happy. She smiled as she walked along the quiet streets, smiled as she ordered her supper in a cheap workers' café, smiled as she caught the last beams of the hot spring sun, smiled when, with a feeling of mild and pleasant exhaustion after a hard day's work, she eventually got into bed.

On Friday she called in at the post office to collect her letters. Much to her surprise there was one there from Semyon Semyonovich. What on earth could he be writing to her about? Could he be ill again? Could it be that he wasn't coming after all ... ?

She was in no hurry to open it, and put it with the others into her leather shoulder-bag. Then she walked through the town until she came to a little square where the birds were singing out cheerful spring songs to each other, and delicate pink almond and apricot blossoms were beginning to appear between the dark fleshy leaves of the evergreens. She sat down on a bench and opened her letters one by one. The first was from her Party friends. They'd been anxious about her, they urged her to return, or at least to get in touch. The tempo of events was quickening and all Party workers should be at their posts.

'Yes, I *shall* go back, the sooner the better, back to my friends, my work, my commitments ... ' She would leave, whatever Senya might say in his letter to her – in fact it might be better if he didn't come at all, so she could leave first thing next morning.

She opened his envelope, secretly hoping he would say he wasn't coming. But no. The moment she'd left he'd poured out his feelings to her in a long and loving letter in which he blamed himself bitterly, told her again and again how much he loved her and assured her that he couldn't live without her. 'Your reproachful eyes have haunted me ever since you left,' he wrote. 'I feel like a criminal and a murderer treating you like that. You can't imagine how precious you are to me, Natasha, more precious than I can tell you. Without you the sun would set forever on my life and the world would be a cold and empty place ... '

At any other time this letter of Senya's would have made her heart race and filled her with almost unbearable happiness. Once she would have covered her face with her hands and repeated his words over and over again to herself, beside herself with joy. But that was in the past. Now she just smiled, a small, patronising smile. 'It's too late,' she thought bitterly, 'now it's too late.' He was counting the hours before he saw her again, he wrote in a postscript. But Natasha was still unmoved. His words simply didn't touch her. It might have been the letter of a stranger. She stuffed it into her bag and hurriedly started reading the others.

One contained a few brief remarks about Vanechka and his Party activities, and she realised guiltily that she still hadn't sent him that postcard. Dear Vanechka, she thought as she wandered away from the square, what a good friend he'd always been to her. She went into a shop, picked out a postcard with a nice picture and pencilled a lighthearted message on the back. She'd be seeing him in a few days, she wrote. She was terribly bored and longed to see them all again, even Dontsov. She knew it was true. She was longing see all her friends again.

On her way back to the hotel she suddenly visualised that terrible hotel at G'ville, the endless corridor, the repulsive carpet, the porter dozing at his table – and herself, in her dressing-gown, her hair tied up in white ribbons, hesitating at Semyon Semyonovich's door, wrestling with her emotions. Standing there like a petitioner. Oh, how loathsome and humiliating it had been! She tried to put it out of her mind.

A telegram was waiting for her at the hotel: 'I'll be there at 1.30 a.m. Meet me!'

'My husband is coming today,' she informed the porter tonelessly and went back to her room. She wanted to make use of these last precious hours of freedom to finish her pamphlet – and most of all, just to enjoy being on her own.

* XVI *

When Natasha arrived at the station, half an hour before the train was due, she saw a message scrawled in chalk on a blackboard announcing that one of the night trains would be late. The porter did not know which one it was, but her question caught the attention of a passing man who, raising his hat politely, told her that a rainstorm had washed away the line, and the train she was waiting for would be forty-five minutes late. As far as he knew there were no casualties. Natasha glanced at him. He was tall, with a small square-cut beard and dark, lively eyes. He seemed most sympathetic. He went on talking. His mother, whom he was meeting, was also travelling on that train. He hadn't seen her for two months. That was too long. He'd really like his mother to live with him permanently. That would be a tremendous joy. 'The only love I can truly respect is a mother's love,' he said, 'because it's the only unselfish love.' He was expansive, like so many southerners. 'And might I ask who madame is waiting for? A friend? Or maybe her husband?'

'Yes, my husband,' she replied, not thinking, then blushed.

'And has madame been married long?'

'That depends from when you start counting.'

'Oh, from before you go up the aisle, naturally – after that, well it's legal but so what? You see, I have my own ideas about this. I'm afraid most women wouldn't agree with me, but as far as I'm concerned there's *pas de différence* whether a woman living with a man is married to him or not. And what's more, I actually think that living with someone you're not married to imposes many more chains than any legal marriage could. I'm not talking about casual extra-marital affairs, of course, I'm talking about morality in important personal relationships. I think it's because a woman must feel so eternally dissatisfied as a man's mistress that she makes such moral demands of him and is so resentful, first with one thing then with another ... Yes, I've passed through that school of experience myself, feeling continually constrained, becoming more and more dependent on your own suffering – oh yes, I could tell you quite a few interesting things about that! Are you German by any chance, madame?'

'No, I'm Russian, and a writer too, so you needn't worry, you can say anything you like to me! Nothing shocks me.'

'Ah, a writer,' he tipped his hat respectfully; 'Now I do respect a woman who has some profession. My mother was a teacher, you know ... But then of course none of that makes any difference in a love relationship – people are still bound to each other by the same emotional chains, don't you agree? No, I really don't believe there can ever be any truth or honesty between a man and a woman. It's just one long mutual lie, an endless pose, a mask, lying for the sake of the other person's peace of mind, lying out of fear, lying because you don't know any better and because that's the only thing you know how to do. Do married people (I mean legally married or in free liaisons) ever have time to be on their own, as single men and women do? Do they ever speak their true feelings to each other? Act on their real desires and needs and moods? Realise what may be the best in themselves? What a joke! No, it's all a game, a mask, a pose and a lie, and that's all there is to it!'

He continued his declamatory speech with abandon, and Natasha understood him perfectly, adding some observations of her own and citing examples to back up what he'd said. 'C'est ça, ç'est ça!' he nodded enthusiastically as Natasha, equally vehemently began pouring out to this complete stranger everything she'd been thinking and suffering these past months. He listened attentively, looking gravely into her face as she talked, occasionally finishing her thought for her with an apt word.

Natasha was the first to realise that the hands of the clock were creeping up to the time when the train was due. Neither of them had noticed how the past hour had flown as they strolled up and down the dingy station platform, deep in conversation.

'I am so very glad, madame, that fate has granted me this happy meeting with you. I do not wish to be immodest and shall not ask your name, but I should like to tell you in all honesty that I have never before met a young woman of such maturity – I say young because it is generally amongst older people that I find such fellow-spirits. Older women don't like talking about these things of course, but there's not much they don't know. Take my mother, for example, a truly remarkable woman. I'm proud to be able to buy her everything she needs now, at the end of her life. What money I have, madame, I've scraped together with my own hands. I'm a wine merchant now but I started off as an errand boy in the cellars and worked my way up from there. My mother was a teacher, and there were eight of us children, all boys. I was my mother's youngest – we never knew our father. Now I'm waiting for the old dear as impatiently as a lover!'

People swarmed on to the platform, as the train drew in. Natasha held out her hand to him. He tipped his hat, leant forward as if to kiss her hand, then thought better of it. Their eyes met. Natasha blushed and withdrew rather fast into the crowd. The train ground to a halt, filling the station with a thick cloud of smoke.

Then Semyon Semyonovich was by her side and hugging her. 'Natasha! How are you? Tired of waiting I expect – but how fresh you look, pink and lovely like a schoolgirl! You must be exhausted, I know I am. This past hour I've been so impatient I could hardly restrain myself from leaping out of the window and racing down the track all the way here!'

Abandoning his habitual caution, he embraced Natasha and kissed her passionately on the lips. Then he took her arm and led her towards the exit, beaming as he recounted how he'd outwitted the professor and given him the slip. 'And now at last, my darling, we can be together, and rest and talk and celebrate our twelfth honeymoon.' He squeezed her arm. 'I'm so happy to see you again, Natasha, so very happy.' She smiled at him, observing him as calmly and coolly as she might observe an innocent child. How strangely remote he seemed to her – never before had she felt this way about him.

At the exit they almost bumped into Natasha's new acquaintance, attentively escorting a white-haired old lady by the arm. Natasha pretended not to notice him, knowing that if she greeted him she would only provoke a lot of unnecessary questions and explanations, tedious suspicions and justifications. But she hated this deception. She knew that by staying silent she was courting her own slavery to another's moods. She'd had enough.

In the car on the way to the hotel Semyon Semyonovich drew Natasha closer to him and sought her lips. 'You can't imagine how much I've missed you, Natasha, and how empty and alone I felt without you. When I saw you looking so unhappy I hated myself and I knew at once what a stupid thing it was to send you away. It was very wrong of me and I'm terribly sorry now. I was just being over-anxious – you know how on edge people can be sometimes when they've been ill, don't you? Do you believe me, and will you ever forgive me?'

'Yes, of course, Senechka.'

'And you're not still angry with me? I don't know, I can't help feeling you're not really pleased to see me. Please Natasha, you must tell me,' he gazed beseechingly into her face. 'Perhaps you no longer love me?' He was almost whispering, as though the terrifying idea had formed itself into words before he'd had time to think.

'No, I don't, I don't love you at all, so there!' Natasha said with a forced little laugh, trying to break the awkwardness between them. But her joke rang hollow in her ears. Semyon Semyonovich sighed and leaned back in a deep brooding silence. Certainly Natasha felt sorry for him, but it was no longer with that sharp, burning compassion compounded of tenderness and respect, which she'd always felt for him in the past. Now she was simply sorry for him as she'd feel sorry for any friend in difficulties.

Eventually she managed to cheer him up by telling him about all the letters from their mutual friends, and in no time he was taking a lively interest in the latest news. By the time they reached the hotel they were just like two colleagues talking over their day's work.

* XVII *

The next morning they got up late; the sun had already left the bedroom when Natasha raised the blind and opened the window. 'Look, Senya, how lovely it is now spring is here.'

'Yes, it's absolutely lovely, what a little paradise you have here.' He came over to the window, put his arm round her shoulder and hugged her. They stood silently together looking out, both of them deep in thought. Natasha felt more at peace than she'd done for a long time. It was as if she were somewhere else, observing it all from a distance. She was beginning to feel a calm and tender sympathy for this dear and extraordinary man who now seemed so very remote from her.

The previous night she responded to his embraces with this same detachment and with none of her usual responsive passion. 'You really ought not to tire yourself out, Senya, you'll only fall ill again. Why don't I tell you what I've seen here instead?' she had urged, trying to distract his attention.

For the first time in their relationship it was *she* who set the mood, treating him rather as one might treat a much younger friend. Before that, she'd always faithfully echoed his moods; now he was following hers without even recognising it. He was happy that Natasha appeared to be so much more contented and – more important – that she wasn't embarking on the sort of long psychological discussions he'd feared she might want to have. He began to feel quite carefree, and wished that things between them could always be as easy as this.

He'd been worrying a lot recently about Natasha's evident unhappiness, although this was something he sensed rather than consciously acknowledged. He didn't understand what its origins were or what he was supposed to do about it, and the more he tried to understand her the worse it became and the more stupidly he felt he was behaving. It had been like this in the past with Anyuta, and now it was beginning to happen more and more frequently with Natasha too. The fault, he felt, must lie with him and his inability to relate sexually to women. A few of his friends were Don Juans, and recently he'd begun to envy them, had even tried to discover the secret of their success.

But now, in B'ere, he felt at last as though he and Natasha were on firm ground again, and the thought that they'd 'found each other again', as she would have put it, filled him with joy. They laughed and joked as they had their breakfast. Semyon Semyonovich greatly enjoyed his rolls and coffee and laughingly assured Natasha that she made a perfect hostess. He was on top of the world. For Natasha it was rather like entertaining an old acquaintance.

'I'd love to stay on a bit longer,' he was saying, 'but unfortunately the library opens again on Tuesday and the professor has invited a colleague of his to show me round the archives. Theoretically I'm free till Tuesday but that means I should really be back by Monday ... '

'Monday, oh that's excellent.'

'Well I don't think it's excellent at all!'

'I do, Senya, because I'm dying to get back – I can't bear sitting around here doing nothing when they're waiting for me at home. This way I'll be able to get back to them by Monday.'

'Why, what nonsense! Why should they be waiting for you? You know they can cope perfectly well on their own. One day more or less is neither here nor there, and I certainly don't see why we should be in such a rush to leave here ... '

'But how *can* you say that in the present political climate?'

'Our friends do exaggerate, as you very well know.'

Natasha said nothing. Even now he was putting his own needs first. In all the years she'd known him he hadn't once offered to sacrifice his time for her, even when she'd entreated him to do so. No, if Anyuta was waiting, then he had to go; that was an iron law, and there'd never been any getting around it. That she too might be in a hurry to return, and that for her, now, every extra day spent here was a wasted one was something he couldn't understand.

'Do you remember, Senya?' she began slowly, thinking aloud, 'that time two years ago when we met in that little town in the north?'

'Yes of course I do. Why?'

'And do you remember how I had a sudden attack of angina? I had a high temperature, I didn't know a soul in that town, it was a horrible hotel ... D'you remember how I asked you to spend just one extra day with me so that I wouldn't have to lie there, all alone, in a strange and uncomfortable hotel? I said to you then: "Just one day, Senechka, that's all I'm asking! What will one day matter to Anyuta when she has you all the rest of the time?" I'd hardly ever begged you for anything, you know, but I was begging you then. But you left all the same, and I stayed there, sick, alone and semi-delirious ... '

'But why are you bringing all this up now, Natasha?' He looked terribly hurt and worried.

'Because when we're discussing *your* arrangements you apparently have no difficulty in understanding that even one day might be important, but when we're discussing *mine* you take absolutely no account of my needs. I find that a strange kind of equality, I must say.' Natasha spoke calmly and unusually coolly.

'How can you say I take no account of your needs, Natashenka? You're quite wrong, my dear, and you know it. Tell me, have I ever forced you to do anything you didn't want to do? No, you're very wide of the mark in your accusations. And if I *have* been doing something wrong, it's really quite unintentional and unconscious. I assure you, *I* want there to be complete equality between us!'

'Well, let's not go into all that now, I expect you're right. Anyway, it's not that important any more. I'm sorry I spoke. I don't know why I said all that.' She tried to change the subject, but Senya responded absent-mindedly and paced about the room deep in thought. Then suddenly his face brightened and he beamed, with that generous childlike smile of his which Natasha had always loved so much. Peering slyly at her over the rim of his glasses, he said. 'Look, I'm going to have a shave now, and then afterwards how about going out to wander around the town together for a bit?' Going up to Natasha, he gazed seriously and tenderly at her, kissed her eyes and hands, then, looking somewhat embarrased, disappeared through the door.

Natasha was baffled. 'Better hurry up, it'll be getting dark soon!' she called out after him.

He was back again in no time. 'That *was* a quick shave,' she said. His mysterious and conspiratorial air made her laugh, for he reminded her of a child with a secret. 'Come on now, tell me what you've done!'

'Guess!'

'Get on with you! How can I guess? Do please tell me, Senechka.' She gave him a playful push.

'I sent a telegram to the professor, so there!' He stuck his tongue out at her.

'Saying what, for god's sake?'

'Saying I'm not going back there until Friday, that's what!'

'Senya!'

He had fully expected that Natasha would throw herself at him and hug him to suffocation in a transport of joy and gratitude. But she didn't; she stood there with her hands at her sides and an expression on her face not of joy but something quite different, an expression which closely resembled rage.

'I see. So without consulting me, or even asking me how I felt about it, you sent a telegram postponing your departure. How could you do such a thing, Senya? How could you just go off and take a decision like that on your own ... ?'

'Natasha, what's the matter with you?'

'I told you Tuesday! You knew perfectly well that I couldn't go back any later than Tuesday!'

'But I only did it because you were so upset when I told you that I had to go back on Monday night. I did it for your sake, Natasha, to show you I *do* care about your feelings, I *do* value you, more than my work, more than anything else in the world ... I thought you'd be so pleased ... '

He looked so crestfallen and injured that Natasha felt she must try to make him understand what she felt. But she checked the impulse. Why bother, when their spirits were no longer in harmony and they had obviously stopped listening to one another? After all, Senechka had longed to do something, anything, to make her happy, and she realised what an enormous concession it was for him to have deferred his departure.

Once Natasha would have been in seventh heaven at such evidence of his love for her. Now she was painfully aware that it was all too late.

She decided to deflect the incident. She would avoid any discussion of her true feelings, for she wanted things to be as easy as possible between them. So she calculated how long her journey back would take, then mildly pointed out that there wasn't enough money for them to consider staying a day longer than Wednesday. Besides, she added, wouldn't it seem highly suspicious to the professor if he stayed on? And then what if Anyuta turned up unannounced in G'ville . . . ?

As she spelt out these possibilities, she felt like a wise mother with years of experience of her child's psychology. She didn't once discuss what *she* wanted, she talked as if she was in no hurry at all to leave, and even thanked him for trying to put her happiness first and offering to stay with her a few more days. Gradually, as she spoke she saw him relax, and when an hour later they stepped out of the hotel to walk arm in arm through the peaceful streets of the old town, she knew he was feeling quite tranquil, elated even.

To her he might have been a sympathetic relative whom she was showing around town, someone with whom she felt happy, not at all bored, someone who is an agreeable but by no means indispensable part of one's life . . .

* XVIII *

'Do you know, Natasha?' Semyon Semyonovich said, closing his suitcase (he was leaving before her), 'I think these have been the happiest days I can remember for many years.'

'Really?'

'I had the impression you felt like that too. True, you have seemed rather strange at times, distant and a bit cold, but as soon as I *listened* to you, as you put it, and tried to be more sensitive to your needs, all that coldness of yours melted. Surely I'm right? Anyway, it's a long time since I've seen you looking so cheerful and laughing such a lot. I shall be able to feel almost good about leaving you ... ' He stopped, pondered a moment, and then, in an uncharacteristic gesture, knelt down before her and buried his head in her lap.

'Senya dear, what is it?'

'I sometimes get these sudden strange feelings, Natasha – I'm terrified of losing you. I tell myself I'm being stupid, but I can't help it. I feel like a little boy who's afraid his mother might abandon him in the dark woods. We're not really getting on very well, are we, Natasha? D'you think we'll become complete strangers to one another? Tell me, Natasha, I must know: do you still love me?'

He gazed at her with anguished eyes, but once again she avoided his question with a laugh. 'Well, this psychologising and self-questioning isn't like you, I'm afraid you must have picked it up from me, my foolish Senya!'

'Yes, you're right, we have reversed roles,' he said quietly, gently stroking her hands. 'This is all very hard for me at the moment, Natasha In a way everything's as it used to be, yet at the same time I sense something different, terrifying. I'm afraid, Natasha.'

Natasha's heart missed a beat. Could it be that now, of all times, when everything was over, he was learning something and was at last beginning to understand her needs, needs which she herself might have been afraid to acknowledge? 'I believe we've experienced too much together over the years ever to become strangers to one another, Senya, and I feel far, far too much for you to stop loving you. But at the moment I see you like a younger brother whom I know and love very deeply, but in a different way.' She stroked that clever head which for so long she had loved to distraction.

'Goodbye, sweet head ... ' A spasm of sadness brought a lump to her throat, and Natasha could no longer check her tears. She sobbed, not for the living Senya she was parting from, but for the end of a dream, the passing of their love and the memory of the joys and anxieties they'd gone through together. Her tears helped her recognise that this was the end. Semyon Semyonovich was consoled by them. 'There, there, nothing's changed,' he hugged her, 'we can still go on as we were before ... ' He picked her up and carried her to the bed.

Natasha stood on the station platform in her hat and veil, her travelling bag slung across her shoulder. Semyon Semyonovich stood on the steps of the train which was about to leave. 'So you go north and I go south, and who knows when we'll meet again? Not for some time, I suppose – these trips of ours cost quite a bit, don't they? But I feel we're only alive when we're together, don't you feel that too? And this time was especially good, don't you think so, Natasha?' He was pleading with her to agree with him.

'Yes, it's a truly heavenly and poetic place, and I shall leave here with a great many new ideas, ideas I've stolen from you, I need hardly say,' She had often flattered him in this way.

'Now don't try currying favour with me, you've a perfectly good head of your own. You'll write to me, won't you Natasha?'

'Of course I will.'

'I'm already beginning to dream of the next time we meet ... '

'Just a minute, I want to check with you whether this is

right,' Natasha interrupted him in a deliberately business-like manner to run over the main outlines of a resolution they'd agreed she would put to the others. The doors were being slammed shut now.

'Goodbye then, Natasha, don't be too miserable,' he stepped out on to the platform to embrace her once more. 'I have so much to thank you for ...'

'For what, Senechka?'

'Everything, my darling. Give me your hand, there, you must go now. The train's leaving. Write to me, sweetheart.' He hung out of the window as the train slowly moved off, and waved his shabby cap at her. Natasha had always found this old cap of his so touching; now she couldn't help noticing how its floppy brim drooped over his face. The train was disappearing into the darkness and the people on the platform were crowding towards the exit, but Natasha didn't move. No anxious peering after the train, as once she would have done. She just felt very peaceful – a little sad perhaps, but not painfully unhappy by any means. Yet she knew that this time they'd parted for good, and that if they ever met again it would be as acquaintances. Of course it was quite possible that, some time in the future, political work might throw them together again. But that would be a meeting of two Party comrades, nothing more. The great love which had made her heart beat all these years, which she thought would never fade, had gone forever. It was dead, extinguished, and nothing, no tenderness, no prayers, not even understanding, could reawaken it. It was too late.

By the time Natasha's train arrived she was no longer thinking about the end of her great love affair with Semyon Semyonovich. She took her seat and at once began to sort through her papers and letters, throwing some away, putting some aside for future reference, replying to others. Now she belonged body and soul to her work. Long, long ago she had felt a great love, but that love had ebbed away. Semyon

Semyonovich, in his heedless, male stupidity, had destroyed it.

So learn from this, all you men who have made women suffer through your blindness, and know that if you injure a woman's heart you will kill her love!

Thirty-Two Pages

and

Conversation Piece

Thirty-Two Pages

* I *

Workshops and factories flashed past, their windows gleaming bright spots in the night, then a row of identical workers' houses, then more houses, an army barracks, and at last the shake and rumble of the railway bridge. As the train finally came to a halt the station lamps cast a little brightness into the murky autumn darkness and lit up her compartment. Footsteps shuffled along the grey platform; the wind danced around the lights, then whistled past into the dark expanse of field beyond the factory wall. She glanced around to check she'd left nothing behind, buttoned up her jacket, stepped out on to the platform and headed for the exit.

Before her stretched an endless empty street lined with barrack-like buildings, twenty or thirty little houses indistinguishable from one another. There were no lights on in the windows, for by now all the workers in this little factory settlement would be asleep. The street lamps flickered. There was no sound.

But as she walked on down the street intermittent sounds, muffled by the distance, did reach her ears, and she recognised the familiar thunder and rumble of the night shift. A dog barked nearby, a shrill nervous bark which made her start. Then she smiled. 'Stop that, stupid dog – it's *me* who's scared!'

She quickened her step and suddenly things didn't seem

nearly so bad. She was probably worrying quite needlessly, forcing herself to make a lot of completely irrelevant decisions. Why should she make any decisions at all, come to that? Nobody else made such heavy weather of their life – why couldn't she be more like other people? Why not simply drop her research and all those important scientific theories of hers? Wash her hands of the whole thing, give it up, move in with him in this little town, stop living for her work and live for love . . . ?

It was out of the question. How could she even contemplate giving up her work, which had so preoccupied her all these months? She sighed and tossed her head, trying to shake off the nagging anxieties which so beset her.

She'd reached the end of the street. On the corner was a teashop, locked up now, its shutters closed, the lamp over the doorway switched off. Could it really be that late? she wondered, stepping under the street lamp and looking at her watch. Yes, it was a quarter past two. She'd have to find some way of passing the time until three, when the night shift ended.

She turned off the road and cut across a piece of wasteland, making for the grey windowless walls of some great unfinished building, and stumbling on to an unmade rubble road. She was beginning to feel very tired.

She turned the corner of the building, and for a moment she was blinded. There, towering over her, flooded with light, panting, clanking and clamouring, stood the factory. One whole wall was crimson with the brightly lit windows of eight workshops. Outside the locked factory gates it was silent and deserted, but inside, behind that dazzling wall of windows, there was a completely different life, one of endless, strenuous work. She could picture the hundreds of figures in their blue work shirts moving about their business with measured concentration, eyes fixed on the work in hand; she imagined conveyor belts rolling, wheels turning, great hammers falling, sharpened steel hissing, hot filings shattering the air with sparks. And she pictured him in there, amongst all those hundreds of figures in their identical blue.

Where exactly would he be? Probably somewhere between the fifth and sixth windows. Would she recognise him, if he were suddenly to come out? She dismissed the thought. How silly. Of course she would. One movement of his hand, the way he turned his head – she'd know him anywhere, for she knew him so well by now that he was already a part of her, and that was why she loved him. What was the expression on his face at this moment, she wondered? Concentration, like the other workers? Or perhaps sadness?

The wall of light cleared before her eyes and suddenly she could see everything inside the workshop as clearly as if she'd walked through the door – she saw the wheels, the belts and the hammers, and the blue figures moving methodically about their business – and she saw him. His face was pinched, and his eyes – what lay behind those eyes? Was he suffering? Did he perhaps know why she'd come today, did he sense that she had finally come to a decision after much anguish and conflict and that she too was suffering?

Maybe. But why couldn't she stop thinking only of *his* unhappiness? What about her own aching sadness, this spectre of the loneliness to come now staring her in the face? And, ah, now she was drowning in the sweet tenderness of her feelings for him . . . !

No, her resolve mustn't weaken. She mustn't look in at the factory window. Forget him working on the machines in there. Ignore the pain in his eyes. Shake off the chains of love and make her own life. No looking back.

She started walking again. That was the way to do it – pursuing her own goal in life, alone, with nobody to stop her or divert her along the way. Walking on as she was walking now, through the darkness, knowing there was a light ahead, knowing there was always her work. It was going to be difficult, she knew that too. It was difficult now, with her feet sinking into the sand at every step, her arms laden with books and shopping bags, the hem of her skirt flapping perpetually about her ankles. But what did all that matter in the end? God knows, it was hard to be alone. But in return she'd have her freedom, in return she'd belong once more to the scientific work she loved and her life would be free of misunderstandings, free of pain, free of arguments. She would no longer be hurt by his failure to listen to her or to value the work she loved – as well as him. Was it possible to love and *not* to suffer? She didn't know. But why shouldn't she try instead to live, and not to love him so desperately any more? She no longer really cared whether or not he listened to her or understood her.

For so long now she'd lived only for the times when they were together, longing only to see him, and convincing herself over and over again that he really did love her. But what had happened to her work in all that time? Nothing! Despite the fact that it was so well planned, so original, she'd made absolutely no progress with it over the past months! She recalled all the times she'd woken up in the morning, her brain burning with the painful knowledge that in the past five months she'd written only thirty-two pages, collected no new material, and hadn't once visited her old professor, her supervisor and her inspiration.

Work steadily and do a bit every day, that was what the professor had advised her. Instead of which she'd done nothing but wait, worry and live only to see her beloved, counting the minutes between meetings, and then returning from her visits drained and distraught, her head empty and her heart full of grief – yes, she could admit it now, grief. And anger that another day had been wasted and still she had only written thirty-two pages.

138

What if she really was incapable of achieving anything, as *he* kept telling her she was? After all, other people managed to get things done in spite of their problems, so why couldn't she? Perhaps this was something all women shared, this conflict between love and work.

These and many other doubts had grown within her over the past weeks, tormenting her, tearing her apart. Terrified of being alone, she had longed for him to be with her to help her forget her fears, and she'd telephoned through to the factory office.

'Hello, has the lunch break started yet? .. It has? .. Well could you ask Pyotr Mikhailovich to come to the phone please? .. Oh darling, is that you? .. Yes. When can we meet? .. You really can't get away today? .. Why not? Too busy? .. Well I'll come and see you then. I'm feeling so wretched without you here ... '

She'd immediately set off on the train to see him. She knew her heart would leap for joy and she'd fling herself into his arms the moment she saw him; then she'd try to tell him how miserable she felt that her work had ground to a halt. Yet she knew perfectly well that the more she struggled to explain herself to him the less she managed to communicate across the chasm that was now separating them. He seemed incapable of listening to her.

Well, he'd say, so what? She should just stop making such a fuss about the whole thing and get on with it – it'd soon sort itself out. The best thing would be if she brought her work with her and moved in with him; that way she wouldn't have to waste so much time travelling to and fro. So she needed the library, did she? Well, she could still visit her precious library. How like a woman, making a lot of fuss about nothing ... And so on and so forth. She knew how it would go.

And she knew too that later, when they'd made love and she was lying in his arms, something would begin to tug at her heart, and she would grow tense. There they'd be, lying so close together, and yet she knew she would feel terribly alone, far, far away from him in a desert of desperation and loneliness, trapped in feelings she hadn't even the words to describe. And they would freeze her heart.

Now, imagining their meeting, knowing full well that once again he would fail to understand her, she could only think that this was somehow because *she* was hurting *him*. And she knew that soon she'd be feeling sorry for him (for he really was so much younger than her in so many ways). Altogether it would be better if she held her tongue when she saw him, and thought more about her work than about him. She'd had enough!

Now that she'd decided to put all her energy into her work, she'd no longer have to suffer his insults and hide her resentment. Time wouldn't hang heavy on her hands any more, for she'd no longer be sacrificing her life, her tenderness, to him. No more counting the hours or killing time, for she had decided to live alone again, and on her own terms. The first thing she must do when she got back was to visit her professor and collect some material. From then on it would be work, work and more work. It wasn't too late – why, her whole life was ahead of her! She could still enrich science with her ideas, as well as making her own small contribution to the new Russia. All it needed was a mighty effort of will – and that meant banishing for a while all thoughts of love and marriage. Her mind was made up, and she knew it must be right, for life suddenly seemed much easier. Her decision even brought with it a kind of happiness. Come what may, she must stick to it. She quickened her step, and soon the factory lights were behind her.

The fresh autumn wind fanned her face and teased the ends of her scarf as she set off across the vast reaped field to the residential part of the town where her lover lived. She shivered with apprehension as she plunged across the field.

She was now enveloped by darkness and chilled to the bone.

For a moment she glanced back regretfully, longing to retrace her steps towards the bright factory she'd left behind ... Perish the thought! How could she be so craven! How could she dream of going back there, simply to wait by the gates till the night shift ended! And really, how childish to be afraid of the dark at her age!

On her right was a sharp slope with a clump of trees at the bottom. What was that rustling sound down there? It must be the wind, she told herself, but it frightened her. What was that, crawling out of the bushes – some person or thing down there ...? Now she was beside herself with terror. There'd be no point in shouting for help, for nobody would hear her. She could still see the factory lights blazing, and *he* would be there, so near, but she knew too that with the din of the machinery he'd never hear her cries. She must walk on quickly and stop dithering on the slope, shivering and frightened to death.

'You're a coward and you're afraid of the dark. So you thought you'd manage on your own, did you? Living alone as an "independent woman"? But there's no such thing! And as for you, you sweet little thing, you're a woman at heart, and you know it ... ' That's what he'd say to her, with that easy laugh of his, and for once he might be right.

She walked on briskly. She mustn't waste time thinking about her fear of the dark; she must think about how she was going to tell him. How would she broach the subject? And when? Today, yes today, the moment they met, the moment he got back to his room after work. But was that really the best time? He'd be worn out and she'd feel so very close to him, so excited to see him again.

'Aha!' he'd say, 'so the runaway housewife has paid me a visit at last! Well, I *have* missed you, love – why on earth didn't you come before? Come on now, confess, tell me what it's all about. But just before you do that ... ' And then her heart would submit so tenderly, and shivering with delight she'd press her body to his and close her eyes ... No, today was quite the wrong time to tell him. Tomorrow would be much better, tomorrow morning.

As she skirted the hill a gust of wind lashed her face, tearing at her hat, stirring the fallen leaves. What a dark and desolate place this was! She turned, heading for the houses, and soon the windows of the factory were mere faint patches of light, the distant rumble faded away. Far ahead she could just make out the lights of the workers' living quarters where his flat was – one small room and a kitchen – but oh, how far she still had to go!

Her legs ached, her arms were weighed down with parcels and shopping bags, and she was now chilled through and through. She cursed the wind, and shrank from the dark bushes which rocked and stretched their gnarled arms out to her. Once again there was that ominous rustling among the leaves, and once again she froze. Suddenly the wind had become some other, nameless force; this waš the terror she had experienced so often in childhood when, alone for the night in her dark nursery, she'd felt 'them' – those fearful, incomprehensible yet lifelike creatures – creeping out of the corners.

It's probably a passer-by, she told herself firmly, or a dog.

The path was narrow, and she kept stumbling. Burdock clung to her skirt. At that moment she'd have given anything to be amongst other people – she longed for the lights and bustle of the town. What had possessed her to come here at night? Why hadn't she had a little more sense and patience? What difference did one day more or less matter anyway – why did it have to be today of all days? She'd been ridiculously over-anxious, unable to focus on anything but her own desperate need to finish with him and lead her own life. She could imagine herself so clearly in her new life, in the room she loved so much, amongst her books and manuscripts, sitting by the lamp at her writing desk, and hearing ...

She stopped dead in her tracks. What was that muffled silvery peal, like a church bell. Where was it coming from? Then she relaxed. Of course, it was just the sound of the railway signal borne on the wind. How stupid of her. She started off again, determined to hurry, but her skirt, flopping about her legs, hampered her every step. She lifted her legs higher so as to lengthen her stride. Her back tingled and she had the sickening sensation that someone was following her and was about to seize hold of her from behind.

She swung round. There was nobody. Utter silence. The air was light and damp, smelling of earth and old leaves and she took several deep breaths. By now the factory lights had disappeared completely.

The wind started up again, but now it became a mysterious night wind, quite unlike the winds of daytime; whipping and whirling, swirling and surging, this wind had sovereign power over the night. It chased long spectral shadows. She couldn't see them but she knew they were there. They were very close too, for couldn't she hear them, rustling and stirring, and couldn't she sense them, retreating, approaching, brushing her as they passed?

She was unspeakably frightened now. There! She felt them again. Yet she could see nothing but the night, thick and stifling. Her leaden feet moved as in a dream. She wanted to shout, but the sound of her own voice terrified her. She wanted to run, but she felt too weak. She wanted to break free of the dark and to escape to a place where there were people and lights – to run, run ... !

Heavy black wings flapped round her head and she was surrounded by something hooting and puffing cold breath in her face. Behind her and all about her now the elongated spectres whirled, touching her, grasping her. Her head would burst – she could endure no more. Air, she needed air. Fiery red and blue circles whirled and leapt before her eyes. A heavy bell boomed and trembled in her ears, flooding the whole earth with its sound. Gasping for breath, she rushed forward, and crashed unconscious to the ground . . .

* II *

'Tell me what happened, love. What've you been up to, fighting again, eh? Well, did someone scare you out there, or did you hurt yourself, or what? Have you sprained your ankle? Tell me why you're crying again – is it because you've been hurt? Tell me where it hurts, then. Come on, don't be so upset, please stop crying now.'

'I'm all right now, honestly; I'm just so happy you're here.'

'Well I should hope I *would* be, you silly thing. Now won't you tell me how you ended up half dead in a field? It's beyond me. There I was, walking home after work, when suddenly I heard this sound in the distance, more of a squeak than a sob really. There's someone being strangled over there, I thought, or maybe it's a suicide or a robbery. So anyway I ran as fast as I could to the spot, and what should I see but this person, huddled on the path and surrounded by a great pile of parcels? Now you tell me the rest. Tell me who frightened you – I've still no idea what happened.'

'Nothing happened. Oh, I'm sorry, but it's true, nothing happened. You see I was just being stupid and suddenly felt terribly afraid of the dark, so I began to run. I thought my heart was going to fail, my head started spinning, and I tripped and fell. But now I'm all right, now you're here – oh how good you are to me, I love you so much – much, much more than you could ever imagine. I'd never leave you, you know that, don't you? Not for anything in the world.'

'Look, stop being so silly – have *I* ever asked you to leave? Oh dear, now you're crying again and I only wanted to comfort you. Now, put your head on my shoulder, that's right, and let me warm your hands – they're like blocks of ice. You just relax now and tell me what happened to you in the field. Please, I must know, were you assaulted?' He peered at her. He was clearly beginning to lose patience, becoming confused and even suspicious.

'But I keep telling you – the whole point is that nobody hurt me and nothing happened, I just ... '

'Oh, come on now, how d'you expect me to believe that, after seeing you sprawled semi-conscious at dead of night, alone in the middle of a field, with your bags all scattered around you and your skirt torn to shreds?'

'All right then, I'll tell you. I'd made up my mind to come and see you immediately and not to wait until the morning, and that was why I was walking to your place in the middle of the night. In fact I'd spent the whole of yesterday steeling myself to do it, because I wanted to try and tell you everything. You see, I can't go on like this any longer. I realise now you don't love me as a friend, nor as a comrade, nor even as just another human being – no, you love me only as a woman, and you simply can't grasp the fact that I need to work, and I need ... No, I just can't bear it any longer.'

'I'm sorry, I don't quite understand.' He spoke coolly, withdrawing slightly from her. 'Perhaps you could tell me just what it is you can't bear any longer?'

'I can't bear us to go on living like this, making each other's lives hell, arguing all the time, never understanding what the other's trying to say ... When I think of all the time and energy we've wasted, all the times I've arrived back from your place feeling utterly exhausted and drained and incapable of putting two thoughts together. D'you realise that in five months I've completed only thirty-two pages of my thesis? When Vera Samsonova wrote the other day to tell me hers was at the typesetters I thought of mine . . . I'll never be allowed to stay on the course if I don't get on and finish it this year, and then that'll be goodbye to all my dreams, goodbye to any future I might have had in science . . . '

'Who's standing in your way then?' His voice remained cool.

'That's not the issue really. The fact is that since we've been together I've spent every moment feeling torn between you and my work – and it's not as if I haven't tried to tell you about my feeling: you don't understand, in fact I think you're deliberately refusing to understand. And now I don't think I can take any more of it. Ah, how easy it would all be if I didn't still love you so much . . . '

'Oh come on, cut it out. You know how I dislike all these meaningless words; it makes no sense to say you love me. When two people are really in love, then they want to live together, spend time together, all that sort of thing – at least that's how we non-scientists understand the word; to you, apparently, it means exactly the opposite. But then I've long given up trying to understand what it is you *do* want. You spend day after day at your place in town, leaving me here alone with nothing to do but my work – it's not as though I didn't have any work of my own to do, you know, and a great deal of it too. And of course I haven't ever said anything about this but, well, I could do with some support from you over *my* work. But that's all by the way. I'm not complaining. I'd hate to stand in your way if you've made up your mind to be a woman scientist. What more is there to say about it?'

'Oh, but I do want you to try and understand me, my love.

It's only because of my work that I feel I can't live here with you.'

'Well let's talk about this work of yours. Will you please tell me why living with me makes it so impossible for you to work? I spend ten hours a day at the factory – you could hardly complain that I'd be around the house all day getting under your feet. Why can't you work at my place?'

'But I have tried to explain that to you, you know. I have to go to lectures and to the laboratory, I need my books and I need the library. I can't work in a camp. I have tried, you know.' Gloomily she shook her head. 'I tried to make a go of it here with you; it was all that damned housework and cooking that made it so impossible.'

'I should think so too! Why should a lady scientist like you have to be doing housework ... '

'Now stop, or you'll make me really angry, and I'm feeling so tired, so fed up with the whole thing.'

'And what about me? *You're* fed up with things – don't you think maybe I'm a bit fed up too? D'you imagine I have an easy time of it with you, having to fall in with *your* wishes all the time?'

'So why in god's name are we dragging on with it like this?' she shouted at him in a sudden frenzy of rage. 'I came to see you today because I wanted to say just that to you, and to tell you I can't go on any longer. All my energy's draining away, and there's no pleasure left in it any more, for you or for me; we're just torturing each other. So let's end it, now! I'm going to leave you ... '

'Leave me then, lead your own life! I can't imagine why you came here to tell me that – what d'you want from me? Did you think I'd throw myself at your feet blubbering and beseeching you to stay? If so, you can damn well think again; I don't go in for that sort of behaviour ... '

'That's a disgusting way to talk, stop it!'

'Disgusting, eh? I suppose you think you're so superior to all that. I suppose you think ... '

'No, I don't think anything and I don't want to either at the moment – I only want you to leave me alone.'

'I'm not even touching you!'

Dawn was glimmering through the window and the oil lamp was burning low. They sat in a brooding and angry silence, alone with their own thoughts.

'All the same though,' he resumed, more gently, 'I would like to know what happened to you out there last night, and about that "decision" of yours – there must be some connection between the two.' Once again she saw the suspicion in his eyes as he glanced at her.

'Look, can't we please change the subject now – I've already *told* you. My nerves are on edge at the moment; I haven't been sleeping well these past few days – I just keep racking my brains for some solution.'

'Oh yes?'

'Why are you looking at me like that, as if you didn't believe a word I said?'

'Well, after seeing you lying there looking absolutely distraught, tears pouring down your face, bags and parcels scattered about you on the ground, you must admit it's a bit hard for me to believe what you say. Wouldn't you like to tell me honestly what happened? All right, I know it's all over between us, but I do still care about you, you know, and if something did happen.... Well it's common knowledge that there are a lot of tramps prowling about these fields. Believe me, I won't think any the worse of you, so please stop lying to me and tell me, like a friend, exactly what happened.'

'What are you suggesting? How ... ? How *dare* you insult me like that? Why do you refuse to understand what I say to you?' She was becoming more and more inarticulate and agitated. 'What sort of a friend are you anyway? You have no respect or sympathy for me. Why do you have to leap to *that* conclusion? Why is that always in your mind? But of course, that's it! Now I understand why I've got to leave you – it's because when you talk down to me in that insulting way of yours I want to run and run and run, far away from you, just like I tried to run away from the ghosts last night. I can't imagine why I still love you ... '

Immediately the words were out he softened. 'Do you mean that honestly? Do you really love me still?'

'But why else d'you think I'd be so unhappy? I've never been so miserable in my life as I have these past few days. Twenty times I made up my mind to leave you, twenty times I thought better of it. One moment I felt I couldn't possibly live without you, the next moment I'd think of my work and your attitudes ... '

'My attitudes to what, for instance?'

'Oh you know, dear, really you do. You don't love me, no you don't, not in the sense in which I understand it anyway.'

'Well I don't know what sense you're referring to,' he said airily, visibly relieved, 'but let's not bother too much about that now. What does bother me, you silly thing, is your strange behaviour. I know you keep trying to convince me you're going to be a scientist and that you're as good as a man and all that, but, despite all that research of yours, you do seem a bit lacking in common sense sometimes, and that does surprise me, I must admit.

'You say you love me, for example, yet in the same breath you say you want to leave me – now what am I to make of that? Don't you think you must be a little soft in the head to come out with something like that? Now madam, look at me with your lovely eyes,' he took her hand, 'and tell me what you're thinking about. Go on, give us a nice smile. So you still love me, do you? What am I going to do with you, eh? I don't know – an intelligent independent woman like

you, afraid of the dark! However did you get in such a panic?
And to think you were going to leave me, when all I want
is to protect you and look after you. I suppose you know deep
down that you couldn't really go through with it ... So why
don't you just snuggle a bit closer and give me a big hug –
I know you love me, of course you do. Honestly I can't think
what this interminable argument has been about, unless you
wanted to torment me for some reason, and yourself too.

'No, on second thoughts, I think perhaps what you *really*
need is to be treated a bit more like a woman – I'm just going
to put my foot down and positively *forbid* you to leave me,
so there! I won't let you go, not for anything, and that's the
end of it. Why don't we both go to your place tomorrow and
collect your books and things, and then you can move in with
me – isn't that a great idea? We'll start all over again and
everything will be fine, you'll see. . . But why are you staring
at me with those great big terrified eyes of yours?'

'No, not terrified.'

'What then?'

'Oh, they're just thinking their own thoughts.'

'Can I ask what about?'

'No point in talking about it really, not now anyway.'

'Well if that's how you feel,' he sighed, 'but I'll never be
able to make you out ... Look it's almost light, you must be
exhausted, we've been talking for hours ... Won't you tell
me what you're thinking?'

'It's really nothing I can put into words, please stop
asking,' she stroked his head tenderly, 'and please don't be
anxious. You're sweet, you know that.' She wanted so much
to ease his pain – he might almost have been her child, for
he was as tough, unthinking and resourceful as a child; and
he certainly loved her in his own way. So why not try to work
things out with him, stay here for a while, postpone her
decision? . . .

'Well then, tomorrow afternoon we'll both go and fetch

your books – we can put up some shelves for them here – and from then on you'll be mistress of this house, how about it eh?'

'Yes, how about it?' But the idea filled her with gloom. Her books ... why, this would mean moving out of her room for good! And what about her thesis? What about the professor? What about the library? It meant goodbye to her work and all hopes of finishing it by January. No, she must escape, find some excuse to go to town alone and escape. Fast. Tomorrow. First thing ...

'Why are you looking so wretched? Why are there tears in your eyes again? Tell me.'

'I'm crying because I still love you, I still love you so very much ... '

Conversation Piece

The man flung open the compartment door at Berlin's Friedrichstrasse Station and stood aside for her as she stepped out. Everything about him – his confident, knowing look, his sensual lips – radiated youthful energy. Unlike her. She was thin and fragile, with untidy dark hair which hung in a long fringe over her anxiously raised eyebrows. Her tired nervous face showed the shadows of experience.

'To think if we hadn't met like this, purely by chance, you'd have slipped off without even saying goodbye to me! You must be the greatest fool I ever met – I can still hardly credit it!' His snappish tone was in direct contrast to the expression in his eyes, which told a very different story. 'To think of all those letters you wrote, telling me how passionately you missed me, how you couldn't live a moment longer without me – and then what d'you do? You run off, just like that, without a word! Why, even common logic should have told you ... '

'Look, I did miss you, oh yes indeed I did, you know that quite well, but won't you try to see my side of things ... ?'

'No I won't, why should I? Now you listen to me instead. You're putting yourself and me through utter hell, and the reason you're doing this to us both is because you're being a fool. All that rubbish about being a "free woman" or whatever it was you called it – a "single woman", was it? Well that all sounds pretty damn silly to me. Be your own

master, is that what you want, eh? Lucky you, is all I can
say. As well as that legally wedded husband of yours who
you get down on bended knee to every day – because that's
what husbands are for, aren't they? – you've got me. And
what d'you want of me? How am I any less of a husband to
you than he is? Tell me that!'
   'Now you're the one who's being stupid, Kotinka. Do
please try and understand. You see, for ten years he and I
have worked very closely together. Emotionally, intellec-
tually, in every way we've been so united. You must realise
how precious that is to me.'
   'All right, all right, there's nothing wrong with that I
suppose – it's just your total enslavement to him I can't
forgive. Look at you, you call yourself a "free woman", you
preach and write about woman's emancipation, and then
suddenly there you are down on your knees saying "forgive
me, Vanechka darling, I've wronged you but I'll promise
never to be unfaithful again".'
   '*Must* you always joke about it?'
   'Actually, I don't see what else I can do in the
circumstances. I suppose I *could* have wrung my hands and
gone into a frenzy of jealous anger over you and your
precious "feelings", but no I thought, better not get too
worked up about it – it's my nature anyway to be fairly
easygoing. So tell me, what is this ideal couple, linked by all
these deep and meaningful spiritual affinities, going to do
next – or shouldn't I ask? I suppose you'll return to him and
beg him to take you back. Then, ever so magnanimously,
he'll accept you, you'll write some more books together,
everything will be exactly as it was in the old days, and you'll
be his grateful servant for the rest of your life. Ah well, you'll
just have to try and trample on all the "guilty dreams" you
used to have about me, over which you used to sigh so
poetically in your letters. You'll have to try and put me
completely out of your mind, won't you? You wouldn't

154

want to recognise me if we meet again sometime, after all. And then there are all those evenings we spent walking in the Tiergarten, you'll have to forget those, you know, not to mention what you describe as my "deadly kisses". And ... '

'Stop it at once, Kotya, stop being so cruel!'

'Aha, so I'm being cruel, am I. Look my love, it's you who are leaving me for your lawful wedded husband with whom you have all those deep spiritual bonds. Remember? It's you who decided you couldn't bear the idea of sacrificing his peace of mind merely for the sake of some young lad who seems to have some deadly hold over you and only knows about loving and kissing. It's you that's leaving me – so don't you call me cruel, all right? Because it's hardly logical.'

He tried to maintain this insouciant tone, but his nervousness was nonetheless very evident. She sat slumped on the station bench, her head bowed. He stood beside her. Both were silent for a moment.

'Kotya?' She looked up, pleading with him.

'Yes?' His eyes met hers.

'Can't you understand – all this really is difficult for me, you know.'

'So what d'you expect me to do – feel sorry for you? Be your ever-sympathetic and faithful follower? No thanks. Look, I did that before, and I'm not going to do it again, understand? I can't think why you don't leave him if this whole thing's making you so unhappy. Go on, be brave, do it! You're an independent woman, you're free, you don't need him. Think how we've loved one another, ever since that first night, think how good it's always been, and just think how you'd melt in my arms this very moment if ... Oh, cut the hypocrisy, my darling foolish woman, and start making your own life again. Why are you doing this to us? What's the point of inflicting all this punishment and suffering on us both? Oh yes, a moment ago I might have been laughing, but how do you imagine I'm feeling inside? How can I bear to let you leave me? Won't you please stay with me tonight and hold me one last time, as you promised you would? Stay with me tonight – then you can decide. Then if you do decide to go back to him, well that's your funeral. But for now, come with me – I've waited for you so long. Morning, noon and night I've waited; the flowers won't bloom until you love me again, so come with me, now. Please. It's little enough to ask of you, when you're going to take away everything I have ... '

'But Kotya, how *can* I? How could I even look him in the eyes when I got back to him? How could I live with myself if I did that? Oh I hate myself, I hate everything.'

'Now everyone's watching you cry – goodness, and you an independent woman too! I think I really believe now what you told me that first night we met, when you said "you're quite wrong about me, you know". Do you remember? "I'm really the most ordinary woman you could possibly imagine, with all kinds of silly prejudices, and your libertine ways don't attract me in the slightest." Aha, so you do remember! And d'you remember how I replied? Yes, you obviously do, because you're grinning all over your face. Well, if you insist on crying in public, I shall employ a time-honoured remedy, right here in front of everyone, and you've only yourself to blame. Oh, so you won't, you coward!'

'No, I won't,' she said firmly! 'I'm not going to compromise myself for you because you're not worth it! I don't care enough about you. Look, there's the Charlottenburg train. Come on, let's hurry and catch it before it leaves. No more discussion now, all right? That can wait – we can see about all that afterwards, after we've said goodbye to one another, for ever ... '

The two figures disappeared into the crowd.